Claire Christian is a novelist and playwright who lives in Brisbane. She has had three plays published by Playlab, and her play *Bloom* was shortlisted for the Griffin Award in 2009. She was one of the YWCA Queensland's 125 leading women in 2013.

claireandpearl.com
facebook.com/claireandpearl
@pearliestpearl

Beautiful Mess

Claire Christian

TEXT PUBLISHING MELBOURNE AUSTRALIA

textpublishing.com.au

The Text Publishing Company
Swann House
22 William Street
Melbourne Victoria 3000
Australia

First published in 2017 by The Text Publishing Company

Book design by Imogen Stubbs
Cover art incorporates images by Shutterstock
Typeset in Sabon 11/15.5 by J&M Typesetting

Printed and bound in Australia by Griffin Press, an Accredited ISO AS/NZS 14001:2004 Environmental Management System printer

National Library of Australia Cataloguing-in-Publication entry
Creator: Christian, Claire, author.
Title: Beautiful mess / by Claire Christian.
ISBN: 9781925498547 (paperback)
ISBN: 9781925410785 (ebook)
Subjects: Friends—Juvenile fiction.
Schools—Juvenile fiction.
Children's stories.

For…
seventeen-year-old Liam,
sixteen-year-old Dave,
fifteen-year-old Steve.

AVA

'We mustn't forget that we here at MacGreggor State College are a community.' Mrs Bryan's triangular eyebrows are so serious below her slick, gelled-back hair. 'And when one of our community members takes a fall we must band together to pick each other up.' She pauses. 'This tree is to act as a reminder of that.'

Then she clears her throat but I don't hear what she says next because I'm screaming. My body jumps out of its seat and my mouth erupts with a yell so violent that I kind of scare myself.

'She didn't fall, she *died*,' I shout. 'She's dead.'

A rolling wave of about seven hundred heads tumble to look right at me.

'And a tree? Are you serious? She hated nature,' I shout up at Mrs Bryan, who is muttering into the microphone for students to take their seats.

I feel angry in a way that I've never felt before, every single one of my internal organs trying to lash out of my body like a rabid security dog, and it's because of what they say about her. Or don't say. It's what they're not saying that pisses me off the most. The past six months I've been able to mainly keep my cool but today when they started talking about the stupid plaque on the stupid piece of concrete next to the stupid fucking tree that's taken them all that time to plant, pretending all like, I don't know, pretending like it's an achievement—pretending like they give a shit—I couldn't take it anymore.

'And if you're going to talk about her at least say her name.'

There is an avalanche of whispers and giggles all around me as Mrs Bryan, yelling now, attempts to calm the hyper masses. I'm stuck in the middle of a row, clambering over the people next to me and muttering like a crazy person. That kid with the spiky fringe pinches me on the arse and I spin and whack his chest, spitting, 'Are you fucking serious?' into his face and I'm pretty sure I see genuine terror fill his tiny blue eyes.

When I finally get to the aisle, to the centre of the heaving groups of students, quieter now but still all staring at me, I freeze.

Do something, Ava.

I look at Mrs Bryan who is staring at me like she wants me dead and I just start to laugh. *Say something, anything, Ava. Stop laughing.* But I can't help it.

I become very aware that I must look like a straight-up lunatic, but I don't care.

I run my hands through my hair, shaking my head as I address the whole auditorium. 'You know what the most insulting part of it all is, though? It's the choir singing that stupid Miley Cyrus song about climbing a fucking mountain in her memory, cause that would've made her want to kill herself all over again.'

The auditorium erupts in laughter and cheers as I give Mrs Bryan the finger with both hands, spin on my heel and march to the back of the room and straight out the two big double doors. I hear them slam behind me.

Way to go, Ava.

I promised myself just this morning that I'd try and be one of those quiet, unassuming girls who blend in. I even scrawled the words *be beige* on the back of my hand in black texta as a reminder. Ever since I've come back to school people have been staring at me, whispering and pointing about as subtly as a sledgehammer to the face. I considered making a shirt with the words *My best friend just died, soz if I make you uncomfortable,* but we ran out of printer ink. Anyway, it seems that leaping out of my chair and screaming at the top of my lungs achieved the same effect.

I've only been back at school full-time for a month, a few weeks part-time before that, and only because I had to. If it was up to me I'd never have come back. I'd have just left with some grand parting gesture like painting a big dick on the oval with grass killer or something. But Mrs Bryan and the other teachers lost their shit about Year 11 and missing work, and my dad was running out of excuses to hold them off any longer. The last few weeks have just fused into a blur of me struggling to pay attention or wagging. Or zoning out when people monologue about how they know how I feel because when their nanna died or when their aunty died or when their fucking dog died they felt blah blah and blah. But none of them know. It wasn't my nan or my aunt or my pet that died, it was Kelly. It was my best friend. There aren't words for how it feels and I don't want to talk about how it feels anyway because everything since it happened, everything right now, is really, really shit and there is no point at all in quadratic equations when my whole body aches with this terrible numb sadness.

It's like life is actually moving slower. I thought school went slow enough before she died. Now it feels like time died right along with her. What makes it worse is that they all act like they're pissed off with me, and with her. They're pissed off with her because it happened and they're pissed off with me because I can't get over the fact it happened. But it's only been six months. That's nothing. I reckon I'm going to feel like this for the rest of my life.

•

When I get to Kelly's house, I open the side gate and walk past the bins into the backyard. Lincoln is sitting on the floor of the patio in nothing but his jocks.

'What are you doing?' I ask.

Lincoln jumps. Sees it's me and relaxes. 'Mum's on my back cause my clothes smell like smoke.'

'So?'

'So now they don't.' He takes a deep drag of his ciggie.

I kick him with my foot and sit down next to him. 'So smart.'

I watch the little movement of his chest as he breathes. His brown skin pulled tight over the muscles in his chest. There's no denying he is hot as. Not like normal handsome, though; more like weird model handsome, like he could be in a surf shop catalogue wearing board shorts and no shirt for sure. He's got a sharp jaw and big brown dramatic eyes which you notice because his hair is always shaved super short.

Lincoln and Kelly's mum, Tina, has been really aggro since Kel died. We used to get on really well. She was pretty much my mum. But maybe a month after the funeral I started to get this feeling she couldn't stand to be around me. Dad reckons it's because I remind her of Kel. Says it must be real hard for her, which I get but I just miss her, miss all of it, the way everything used to be. I can only come around now when she's not home. If Tina found me here she'd freak out, and if she found out about Lincoln and me I think she'd completely lose it. I don't want to upset her, but I can't help it. I like being here; the smell of their house is so familiar to me, like coconut oil and lavender and dust all mixed together. I know where they keep everything in the kitchen, and where to step on the wooden floorboards so they don't creak. I feel less crazy when I'm here, which in itself is crazy because everything at their house at the moment is absolutely nuts.

'You weren't at school,' I say. I notice now when he's not around, I never used to.

'Nah.' He pauses for a second before he says, 'But I heard you were.'

Of course he bloody did. I exhale loudly and turn away from him, rubbing my forehead with my hand.

'You want to. Talk. About it?'

'Lincoln, you don't want to talk about it.'

'Nah. But do you?'

'No,' I say quickly. I don't want to talk about it now because I'm going to have to keep talking about it. I'm going to have to go through it with Dad, and the principal and the school counsellor and every dickhead kid at school that looks at me like an idiot for the next few weeks. I take the cigarette out of his fingers and inhale deeply. There's a long silence before either of us speaks.

We've always got along, but we were never friends. I mean, I was pretty much here every weekend since I was about four, and I went on most of their family holidays. But Lincoln was just always the cool older brother, fixing bikes or playing loud music or drinking in the garage with his mates.

When we were younger we would spy on them from the backyard. We figured if we knew what boys talked about when girls weren't around then we'd be better equipped to talk to them when we were around.

When we were in Year 9 we started to go to the

same parties and I think that freaked him out a bit. Kel would hook up with his friends and he'd flip out about it, real protective, and him and Kel would fight about it and he'd say, 'That's just the way it is, Kelly. I'm older therefore I know better.'

But Kel wouldn't have taken that from anyone and especially not Lincoln. She made up this rule that he wasn't allowed to hook up with anyone in our grade and she wouldn't hook up with anyone in his and both of them were keeping their end of the deal until the night we all went to Stuart Gillespie's eighteenth. Lincoln really wanted to hook up with Amanda Higgins, who has massive boobs. Like porno massive.

'Fuck the deal, Kel, Amanda's so up for it, ay?' Lincoln said, standing right in front of Kel, shifting his weight from one leg to the other like one of the netball girls so Kelly couldn't get past.

'You're a pig,' Kelly scowled.

'Come on, just this once?'

'If you hook up with Amanda I'm going to make out with...' she looked around the party scanning the guys. 'Tom Greig.'

Lincoln scoffed loudly. 'He's a dick.'

'You're a dick,' Kelly snapped back.

Lincoln groaned, looked over at Tom Greig, who was cheering as some other guy sculled from a bottle of vodka. 'Fine,' he mumbled as he walked away. Then he turned back and looked right at me. 'And who are you going to hook up with, Aves?'

I just stood there stunned. 'No one,' I mumbled. 'No

one.' This time trying to seem more confident.

'Yeah.' He paused. 'Probably not that many guys here who'd hook up with you anyway.' And then he walked off with Kelly yelling at him to get fucked.

She quickly spun back to look at me. 'He didn't mean that, Aves, he's just trying to piss me off. All the guys here'd be lucky to make out with you.' Her face cracked with her enormous teeth-filled grin and I couldn't help but laugh. She leaned her forehead on mine so her eyes kind of mushed into one because she was so close. 'You're the most beautiful of them all,' she whispered and I just nodded. She always knew exactly what to say. Always.

Right after it happened Lincoln and I started texting, mostly about the stupid shit that people would say or do, and then we started hanging out and then we—well, yeah. I figure he's the only one who really actually gets how I feel. Kind of. I don't even know if I like him like that, even now, after everything that's happened between us.

'Wanna get stoned?' Lincoln asks. I shake my head. I don't. 'Wanna'—he pauses and looks at me with his big brown eyes and takes a deep breath—'root?'

'God, Lincoln.' I shake my head, smiling. 'Who says root?' He doesn't move his hand, he leaves it lightly on my neck and he smiles at me.

'What do you want?'

I exhale again and lean my head on his shoulder; he lifts his arm and puts it around me. I feel Lincoln kiss my forehead and I gulp down the large lump in my throat. Lincoln looks at me, right in the eye and neither of us moves for what I reckon is a whole minute. We just sit there looking at each other. I've never been able to hold eye contact with anyone but it's like with Lincoln I'm not even nervous. Not like how I feel with other guys. I've had boyfriends and that, nothing serious, but it was always Kel who would make it happen. She was confident, especially with people she liked. She kissed whoever she wanted to kiss and she'd make whoever she liked like her back. She'd also make whoever I liked like me. It was a pretty sweet pay-off.

There's very little we didn't do together. We even lost our virginity on the same night, in the same house, pretty much at the same time because that's what we'd planned. Ahmed was a sweet Muslim boy who had just graduated from our school and I thought he was the loveliest. He played violin in the school string quartet and he was going to uni to be an engineer. We'd talk online most nights about homework, life, our future and stuff and when he saw me at school he'd always make an effort to say hello to me. He didn't really go to parties so I didn't see him much outside of school. His best mate Jack played rugby. He was a big dude, really funny and really sweet; he'd turned eighteen right at the beginning of Year 12 so he'd instantly become one of the most popular kids at school because he'd buy everyone's booze on the weekends. Kel liked Jack and so we all shared a bottle of Galliano and Kelly asked Jack to show her his room, which left Ahmed and me alone in the lounge room frozen, neither of us able to work out what to say until finally he muttered, 'Do you want to see the spare room?'

I nodded and we walked up to the hallway in silence. The awkwardness was agony so as soon as we got to the spare room I kissed him so we'd have something to do and we wouldn't have to endure the silence any longer. We didn't really talk while it was happening, we just did it. I don't know why, probably because we thought we should, because Jack and Kelly were in the other room doing it, and it was easier to just do it than explain why we hadn't. It was fine. I mean it wasn't bad, it just happened, nothing like in the movies where it's crazy romantic or passionate or anything, just quick. A non-event, really.

With Lincoln it's different. It's better. It's fun. Most of the time.

'Hosana sent me the video of you today.' Lincoln laughs and I look up briefly before burying my head into his shoulder, mortified. My crazy-lady outburst online forever. Great. 'I cracked up laughing when you gave Mrs Bryan the finger. He'd zoomed in on her face and it looks like she's actually gonna spew.'

I groan. 'Do I look completely mental?'

'Nah, you look cute as,' he lies. I smile, whacking him on the leg and he grabs my hand and squeezes it.

'They just make me so mad.'

'Yeah, Aves. I know.'

Flirting with Lincoln makes me feel better about

what's about to happen. Maybe he feels the same way. I don't even know if he likes me. I mean he must a little, but not like that. I just know that when I hang out with Lincoln everything else doesn't matter as much. What happened at school today doesn't matter. What my dad will say later doesn't matter. Being with Lincoln makes me forget how messed up everything else is. Or maybe forget is too strong, maybe he just makes me feel something other than shit for a bit. Like I used to feel when Kelly was still alive. Which is weird because this never would've happened if Kelly was alive.

'Come on,' Lincoln raises his eyebrows at me and stands up. He doesn't say anything as he leads me through the sliding door, up the hallway, past Kel's closed bedroom door, into his room and onto his bed.

•

It's dark by the time I get home.

'Where have you been?' Dad shouts from the kitchen the second I walk through the door.

'Kel's.'

'Ava!' Dad appears with a tea towel over his shoulder and a scowl on his face. His floppy grey hair bounces as he shakes his head. 'I thought we agreed you wouldn't go there.'

'Yeah we did, but Lincoln wasn't at school today so I wanted to see if he was okay,' I lie, and watch Dad's face as it crinkles into a smirk.

'Bullshit, kiddo.' He turns and walks back into the kitchen. I kick my shoes off and follow him.

*

My mum left us the first time when I was about six months old—she dropped me in the reception area of Dad's office and left. We didn't hear anything from her for like, two years when she just showed up on our front stairs in a panel van. She hung around for a bit and then left a note on our coffee table that said *I'll call you*, and pissed off overseas.

That was her longest stint away because we didn't actually see her again until I was nine. She'd write post-cards from Paris, Berlin, Lithuania, Egypt and she'd never sign them *Mum*, always *Barb xx*. Never any regularity; just whenever she felt like it.

Her and Dad fell in love quickly, got married and had me all in like twelve months. She must have just been in one of her manic phases, where she comes across all flighty and free-spirited like a real gypsy. But on her other days, her low days, she's dark and moody, she lies and she is mean.

My relationship with my mum is nonexistent, really. I think about her like you do a distant relative. I feel like I know her based on what my dad has told me or from these quick bursts of interest she shows in me. We don't have anything in common apart from genes. I reckon if I met her and didn't know her I still wouldn't like her, and I'm okay about it.

I've seen what she's done to Dad and I used to really care, wanted her to be around, didn't understand it. I still don't but I guess I've just got used to it. I haven't seen her for a year; she's living in Darwin. She got married to some guy with long hair and sent me a photo. She never had another kid.

'What's for dinner?'

'Don't change the subject. You had a shit day?' He's got his back to me, stirring whatever is on the stovetop. He says the last part like it's both a statement and a question. Like he knows I had a shit day, but like he also wants to know if it really was a shit day.

'Did school call?'

'Yup.'

'Why didn't you call me?' I ask.

'Because I knew you'd tell me about it.'

He's right, I will. I'll tell him about the stupid speech and my ranting. I'll tell him about storming out and going to Lincoln's. I obviously won't tell him what Lincoln and I spent most of the afternoon doing, but he'll get the idea. Dad and I have always been able to talk but before there'd always be parts of the story missing. We were on a need-to-know basis and to be honest, there was a lot of stuff that Dad didn't need to know. Like I'd tell him I was going to a party but I wouldn't tell him I would be drinking. I'd tell him I was going out with a guy, but I wouldn't tell him I was going to stay at his place. Don't ask, don't tell—it worked for us. But since Kel died we really talk, like no-bullshit talk. I tell him what's going on and he listens and he tells me what he thinks and very rarely does he get weird.

After dinner, after we've sat at the bench talking about the day, he says, 'What about Lincoln?'

He reaches over for my plate. Looks at the spag bol he made and furrows his brow. I haven't really eaten much, just kind of pushed it around the plate.

'What about him?'

'What's going on there?'

'I dunno,' I say and I don't know. I don't know why every time I see Lincoln now we hook up. I don't know why we get stoned. I don't know why, when we see each other, we pretend like nothing has happened and I don't know why we never talk about Kel. I don't know.

'Just—' Dad stops himself. 'Just be careful.'

'Yeah.' I bite my lip and the usual wash of guilt floods my body.

'You just need to think about the fact that things aren't...' He pauses and breathes in, searching for the right word. 'Things aren't typical right now. Lincoln is navigating some pretty big things and he might just... he's not himself.'

I rest my elbows on the bench and rub my temples with my knuckles, leaning into my hands.

'That's just it, though. That's how I feel when I'm there.' I look at Dad standing at the sink. 'Myself.'

He looks at me for a really long time. His lips move like he's about to say something but he doesn't, he just nods.

'I hate it, Dad.'

'I know.'

When I was little I was never allowed to say I hated anything. My dad hates the word hate. So if I really didn't like something I'd have to say that I immensely disliked it. 'I hate broccoli,' I'd say and Dad would go, 'No, you don't hate broccoli, you immensely dislike broccoli.' Obviously, Mum and Dad had a confusing, messy, just-shit relationship, mainly cause she was a bitch. He hated her. Not so much anymore, he's moved on, but he hated her then and he had reason to. He knows what real hate feels like: the rage, the intensity, the vile anger that blacks out everything good and real, eliminating your very sense of yourself. He had felt that. So, the way I felt about broccoli was very different to the way he felt about my mum. By setting that as the bar, the way my dad felt about my mum, I suppose I've never really hated anything.

Until now. I hate what Kelly did. I hate that she left me on my own.

GIDEON

I write poems.

But there's no way to say that without sounding like a dickhead. I've tried. I spend a considerable amount of time trying not to sound like a dickhead. That's what my life is—trying to not sound like a dickhead and overcompensating for moments when I'm positive I do sound like a dickhead, like right now. I'm pretty sure I sound like a dickhead right now.

I write slam poems.

Saying this doesn't work either, mostly because people don't know what slam poetry is and when they ask I just end up rambling about the origin and evolution of spoken-word poetry around the world. In case you were curious, a surefire way to look like a dickhead is to be a lanky white kid babbling about the revitalisation of poetry in America in the late 1980s.

This is why, instead, I choose to stay quiet in most public situations and why I choose to write rather than concern myself with real-life conversations, because it's easier. You can fix your mistakes, even delete things entirely. You can make yourself sound smart or artistic or a whole array of other descriptive words. One of which is not 'dickhead'.

I wriggle the too-tight knot of my tie and stare at the back of the cubicle door. Try to catch my breath and calm myself down. I've worked myself into such a tizzy thinking about what questions they're going to ask me that I'm about four laboured breaths away from being asphyxiated by my own oesophagus.

I'd like to avoid that. I stare at the print ad on the back of the door and wiggle my toes. I don't know why wiggling your toes is meant to help but that's what the parental unit always tell me to do. So I do. I think it's meant to make me focus on something other than the impending doom that looms like a shadow in my periphery. *Don't focus on the shadow*, I repeat over and over again. *Don't* focus on the shadow. Don't focus on the *shadow*. Focus on wriggling your toes. Focus on the ad.

Compartmentalise. Good.

With my toes wriggling madly inside my tight brown leather lace-ups I stare at the ad, at the lady in the short black skirt and red high heels. She's standing over some guy in a suit who's sitting down on the floor with an expression of cartoon confusion on his face.

The lady in the heels rests a broom on his chest and there is a caption in big swirly red lettering; *Don't get swept up with nerves. Be the man she wants you to be.*

It takes me a couple of minutes to work out that it's advertising erectile dysfunction spray. But staring at her collarbones and the extremely perky boobs that poke studiedly above her strapless top confirms a couple of things for me. Enough things to make a list:

THINGS I KNOW RIGHT NOW: A LIST

1. I'm having a bit of a panic attack.
2. I have a slight erection.
3. I don't need to call the number on the poster for men who suffer erectile dysfunction.
4. I write poems.
5. And, evidently, lists.

I close my eyes and try to think of breathing, just breathing. I try not to think about how stupid all of this feels, how stupid I feel. All of this because of a stupid job interview. A stupid job interview at a stupid menswear store where I would've had to help men like the ones in the picture who probably do need erectile dysfunction spray. At least I don't need the erectile dysfunction spray, silver linings, although I wish there was such a thing as just plain old dysfunction spray. That'd come in handy right about now.

I feel my heart rate drop from the spheres of catastrophe and land somewhere in a realm closer to normal and I read the caption again.

Don't get swept up with nerves. Be the man she wants you to be.

But that's just it, attractive woman in your incredibly short skirt; you want me to be the kind of man who has erections and knows what to do with them. A guy with a nice haircut and some sort of muscle tone who isn't intimidated by anyone or anything, especially not job interviews.

I put the toilet lid down and sit. I'm not that guy. Not even a little bit. I'm the kind of seventeen-year-old guy who gets nervous most of the time, who uses words like 'tizzy' and who works himself into tizzies over dumb things like job interviews, or any situation for that matter, that require him to talk about himself. I'm the kind of guy who gets turned on by a cartoon of a beautiful woman but who'd rather hide in his bedroom alone than have sufficient interactions with beautiful women so that he could ever be turned on by them in real life. I'm the kind of guy who has panic attacks in toilets.

I look at my watch.

I'm the kind of guy who ends up being late to job interviews. The kind of guy who, because they're late, they just won't show up to job interviews but will tell their parents they did. The kind of guy who will tell his parents that the job interview was fine, who won't tell his parents he missed the job interview altogether because of things like panic attacks or erections or because he got stuck in a toilet cubicle thinking about what kind of guy he is.

•

'Which means that life is…' Robbie, my therapist, asks and I shrug. I've been seeing Robbie since we moved here. He was the fourth therapist I saw. The other three were old, frustrating or patronising. He wasn't. Robbie looks nothing like a 'typical' therapist; he's a bit fat, has a beard and he's clinging eagerly to a ponytail despite going bald. He wears jeans and T-shirts. He's the reason I got into poetry. He is like no one I know.

When I first met him he asked me a heap of quick questions like what my favourite movie and food and subject at school was. He asked if I had a girlfriend or a boyfriend, and I shook my head, embarrassed. But I liked that he didn't assume anything about my sexuality, because I figured that would mean he wouldn't assume anything else about me. All I'd ever experienced up to that point was people assuming things about me because of what I said, or wore, because my mums were gay, because of my scars. Robbie didn't. He still doesn't. He told me he wouldn't be offended if I didn't like him or if I didn't come back, because some things just weren't meant to be.

'So, Gideon, this is where we get to know each other a bit,' he'd chimed, resting his hands on his big belly. He stood up and got two cans of Coke out of the tiny fridge next to his desk and placed them on the coffee table between us. Tick two for Robbie. For the last few months my mums had been obsessed with my diet. No sugar. None. They even made our own toothpaste because Mum had read something about sugar in commercial toothpaste. Thankfully this phase didn't last too long, but that can of Coke was like the first hit of smack for an incarcerated drug addict. The point is, the Coke was a gesture, and one that made Robbie cool in my slightly warped, sugarless thirteen-year-old brain. We spent the rest of that first session just talking about what celebrities we thought were hot. I told him that I wasn't really attracted to any of the women in *Friends* and he told me I'd never understand. He made me laugh. Tick three for Robbie. He didn't ask me once about antidepressants or self-harm or depression or hospitals or bullying or my feelings. Unless they were my feelings about *The Simpsons* versus *South Park*. *South Park*, obviously. Robbie picked *The Simpsons* and then scoffed about how he had T-shirts older than me.

Four years later Robbie is still my therapist.

'And that means life is…' He smiles and asks again. I am so used to this conversation, but it doesn't make it any easier to answer. I already told him about the toilet cubicle incident, which admittedly he'd laughed about before he told me that I'd dodged a bullet by failing to land a job in menswear.

'Life is the same. But,' I pause and Robbie raises his eyebrows, waiting, 'I'm over it.'

'Explain.' A touch of alarm sounds in his voice.

'Not *life*. No. Shit, Robbie. I'm just over everything being the same.'

'Okay.'

I take a deep breath, and stare at the old movie posters on the wall. 'I'm bored,' I finally say without thinking, and as soon as I say it it's like I've shone one of those giant spotlights on my feelings. I'm bored. I'm so bored of everything, of being careful, of being nervous, of overthinking everything, of locking myself in toilets.

'The worst quandary of them all, my friend,' Robbie puts on a weird accent. 'They say that death kills you, but death doesn't kill you, boredom and indifference kill you.' I look at him and he smiles. 'Who said that?' he asks.

'Gandhi?'

'Close. Iggy Pop.'

'Who?' I ask and he throws his pencil at me.

'I want you to think about small risks, safe risks, things that are going to push you out of your comfort zone. Sometimes the smallest things are enough to spark a fire or set you on a whole new path or some other wanky metaphor, yeah?'

'I need to get a job,' I nod. Robbie is right. Robbie is always right.

'What kind of job?'

'Anything. I need cash.'

'For illicit substances, booze and ladies of the night? I know all about you youth.' Robbie chuckles at his own joke. 'Well, let's talk about your CV.'

'Lanky, introverted, awkward poet with big hair and questionable fashion sense requires well-paying job to fund awkward, introverted activities,' I say.

'So, something in customer service then?'

•

'Gideon, you need to settle this argument.' My mum, Mandy, is standing on a ladder in the lounge room holding the iPad up to her face. Her blonde bob swishes as she turns the screen around and my sister Annie pokes her tongue out at me. I drop my schoolbag and give her the finger with both hands dancing at her. Mum and Annie are laughing as Susan, my other mum, walks in behind me, copying the double-middle-finger dance. She wraps her arm around my shoulder. 'It's not an argument, it's a conspiracy. Your sister and your mother are ganging up on me,' she pauses, 'as usual.'

Cue raucous mockery from Annie and Mum about how she's so hard done by and it's not a conspiracy and she just has awful taste. The point of the issue is two large squares of wallpaper that have been stuck up above our redundant fireplace. 'Which one, buddy boy?' Mum points to both like a game show host as Susan takes the iPad and blows Annie a kiss on her way back to the couch. I go to stand by the ladder and ponder two strikingly similar swirling patterns: one is green with silver swirls and the other silver with green swirls.

'I like the silver one,' I say as Susan leaps off the couch and hugs me.

'I knew my boy had good taste.'

'Two against two,' Mum smirks. 'Let's leave them both up and reconvene this meeting in a week.' She steps down off the ladder and wraps her arm around my waist.

The rest of the conversation with Annie lasts a couple more minutes as she shows us how gross and rainy it is outside her London window. Annie is two years older than me and she's the smartest person I know. She got dux of the school and all of these scholarships to all these different universities which she politely declined to go work in a pub and travel around Europe. Annie is fiercely opinionated and political; she loves maths, paints big murals with pastels and funded her whole trip to Europe by joining one of her friends' dad's pyramid scheme when she was fifteen. Annie is super entrepreneurial and business savvy. When she was eight she ran this serious tuckshop mob ring at school, where she would buy lollies with her weekly pocket money and then bag them up and sell them for a profit next to the tuckshop. She made a mint. Pun intended. It would've kept going except one of the mums caught wind of what she was doing and the school shut it down. I miss her every single day.

My family is a little abnormal in that we all genuinely like each other. Also, my parents are still noticeably very much in love, even though they've been together like forever. They celebrated their twenty-fifth anniversary last year so Annie and I threw them a big surprise party in the backyard; they both got really drunk and went skinny-dipping in the pool. So it was a massive success.

I go up to my room, put my favourite record on the player and sit on the edge of the bed and I start to think about what small, safe risks might look like. Robbie and I talked about a few: handing out résumés to local shops, entering more poetry competitions, talking to new people. Maybe reconnecting some of the electronic devices I got rid of six weeks ago, all my game consoles, my laptop and my phone. Not that I really used my phone. You need to have friends to use a phone, and the only friends I have are Norma and Andy. I told myself I'd go twelve weeks without any device. Just to see. It was all sparked by a stupid comment on a photo, a photo at the sports carnival of four people in my grade hugging and smiling and me all tiny and pixelated walking across the oval in the background. Some guy had then commented with three words:

Whose that kid?

It wasn't the comment itself, really, more the fact that it acted like some kind of skipped stone in a pond of really shit memories of how I used to feel and why we ended up moving. It dredged up memories of all the things that had happened. I don't want to feel any of that again so I got rid of it all. Just to see. And life has stayed the same.

Maybe being bored is a good thing. Because what that actually means is that things aren't like they were. And that's all I ever really want, for things to never be like they were.

AVA

There's a stabbing pain in my forehead. My eyelids open just a crack and a bad feeling washes over me. Part confusion, part dread, it's a feeling I've become all too used to lately. It starts like a tsunami at the top of my skull, crashes through my insides and stops at my feet. It forces me to sit up and look around.

I'm on an airbed in what looks like a home office. It's the morning and it's quiet, just the low roar of cars changing gears and birds.

My heart skips double beats: I'm not alone. There's a shirtless guy asleep on the airbed with his head underneath a pillow.

I close my eyes. *Think, Ava, think.*

My mouth is dry and it's hard to swallow and I look down. I'm still wearing my dress from last night and a jacket, a guy's jacket. Lincoln's jacket. I lift up the pillow and the guy groans, moving his head to face me with his eyes crinkled shut, and it's Lincoln.

I breathe out loudly through my nose. Lincoln lifts his arm and uses the smallest amount of pressure to push me back down so I'm lying next to him.

'Go to sleep, Ava.'

'Where are we?'

'We're sleeping,' he mumbles. He still hasn't opened his eyes.

I lie as still as I can and bite my lip trying to remember what happened last night. Lincoln picked me up from the petrol station at the end of my street so my dad wouldn't know. All week Dad had been trying to talk about grief-based choices and looking after myself. Each time I'd just tune out and nod. We went to Travis Deakin's party and it was lame, so we left. Lincoln stole a bottle of Johnnie Walker from inside the house and we walked all the way over to MacGreggor Park, drinking and talking shit, sitting in the old graffitied egg thing that spins around, kissing, making out for ages. And then me deciding that I most definitely did not want to have sex in the spinning egg in the park, because Lincoln totally would have if I'd have wanted to.

I stare at the ceiling and all my guts twist and tense with embarrassment, and then gratitude. I'm grateful that drunk Ava is occasionally capable of making the right call. I've done a fair amount of stupid shit in the grip of 'grief-based choices' lately but I'm glad I don't have to add having sex in a playground to the list.

I remember telling Lincoln I wanted to do something fun and him saying, 'Aren't we doing something fun?' before I stood up too quickly, which made the egg spin and me fall out, landing hard on my hands and knees. I look at my hands. They're puffy and red and they sting from the bits of gravel and sand still in them. My knees too, covered in dried blood where I've met with something sharp.

I remember Lincoln piggybacking me through the park and then getting a phone call about some other party. Him rolling a joint and us walking for what felt like hours and how he tried to hold my hand but it hurt so I pushed him away and he got pissed off with me. Then I remember screaming at him in the street and crying. Messy loud crying and him trying to get me to be quiet, and holding me as I pushed him away.

I remember getting to some guy's house who I didn't know and feeling really shit and drunk and stoned and sick and telling Lincoln to take me home.

I turn my head and look at him. He's sound asleep and breathing through his nose. His eyelashes are so long. I feel nauseous and sad. It's pretty much how I've felt since it happened.

Ever since Kelly and Lincoln's dad rang my dad at 5:37 a.m. I know because they called the house phone; it woke me up and I immediately checked the time. Seven minutes later Dad came into my room and whispered, 'Aves, are you awake?' I knew immediately that something wasn't right but I thought something must have happened to my grandparents because Dad's eyes were full of tears that had just started to spill onto his cheeks. I sat up and stared at him and he swallowed so hard that I could see the muscles in his throat move. It was like everything slowed down waiting for him to tell me that something had happened to my Yiayia, so when he finally said her name, when he finally said, 'Kelly has—'

It was a wrecking ball to everything in my life up until that point. I couldn't move. Couldn't really hear what he was saying, just the rush of my brain whirring, liquidising, dropping down into my heart, making it so heavy it broke. Only my heart didn't just break, it shattered. Complete oblivion. She died. That's all he said.

'Kelly has—Aves. She died.'

She died thirty-one Sundays ago. I know because I've counted. And now, every Sunday feels like this. Starts like this. All thirty-one of them.

•

My hand's wrapped in ridiculously obvious bandages because of my stupid drunken stack on Saturday night. The left one is infected. I had to go to the doctor and get antibiotics and then another lecture from Dad about me basically not being a dick anymore.

'I know you're hurting. I'm hurting too,' he said. 'It hurts. But you're not an idiot, Ava. Don't start acting like an idiot now because you're sad. Life goes on, kiddo. You've got to find a way.'

Part of me knows he's right, I have been acting like an idiot, but the other part of me is just pissed off with him for not understanding. For making out like I should know how to behave when my best friend dies. I feel like I'm doing the best I can just by gritting my teeth and getting on with it. In fact I'm pretty bloody proud of myself and how I've managed these last few months, because if you'd told me that Kelly was going to die I probably would've told you that I would've died too. In some ways I think I have. Parts of me, anyway.

'Why am I paying you if you can't even work today?' Ricky's shaking his head as he looks at my bandaged hands. I can't get them wet, which also conveniently means I can't wash any of the gross salad buckets in the sink, or hose the floors or clear the drains.

Before this year, the thing that would make me the saddest was if I was rostered to work on a Friday or Saturday night, because working at Magic Kebab on a Friday or Saturday night is its own special kind of hell. Drunk people yelling stupid shit about ridiculous things, being obnoxious and gross. Guaranteed some girl in a micro skirt would spew at the entrance and then try and fight another girl, holding her glittery heels in her hand. While their disgusting boyfriends stand on the side and make dumb comments about joining in.

If I had a dollar for every time a meathead guy said the words, 'Smile, beautiful,' to me...Well, I'd no longer have to work weekends at Magic freaking Kebab.

There are some highlights, though. Like Ricky, who inherited the business from his dad and is the funniest person I know. Dead set. Ricky has a dickhead policy.

The dickhead policy is simple because there are two levels of dickhead: 'Class A dickheads' and 'Class B dickheads'. If you are a Class A dickhead we fill your kebab with jalapenos or Ricky's homemade hot chilli sauce. The pleasure of watching stupid drunk girls with their tongues lolling out trying to work out why their faces are on fire is totally my favourite thing ever. Class B dickheads just get charged more. Ricky always works the till and he adds an extra '0' to their order. So their $8.50 kebab costs them $85.00. They never realise. Ever. On those nights Ricky gives us cash-in-hand tips.

Okay, so maybe Magic Kebab isn't actually that bad.

When Kel died, I found a bottle of homemade chilli sauce on my doorstep with a note that read: *For the dickheads. Love Ricky.*

'Because you love me,' I say to him now.

'It's true.' Ricky pauses, his big round face nodding as beads of sweat roll down the sides of his moustache. 'Now clean the windows.' With one swift push he jams a bottle of window cleaner in my hand and struts off humming.

I like cleaning windows. And mirrors. It's a weird sense of satisfaction because it's really clear if you've done a good job. Like actually bloody clear. So many things in life don't feel like that. Especially at school where there are contradictions all the time. They want you to speak up for yourself, but only if you say what they want to hear. They're constantly talking about maturity and us behaving our age but then they're trying to make us choose what we want to do for the rest of our life right now. It's so dumb.

Dad and I had to sit in Mrs Bryan's office the other day while she told me that all of the staff and students were concerned for me and how they really wanted to do everything in their power to help, but only if I stuck to the school rules and behaved like nothing had happened and didn't tell everyone to get fucked in assembly. She made it clear she was doing me a favour by not taking further action for my emotional outburst. Then she told me I needed counselling. Dad sat quietly, taking it all in. Occasionally apologising or thanking her for understanding or explaining that *we're doing our best to navigate this difficult time.*

I just sat with my arms folded, scoffing at all the bullshit. They don't know what to do. The school keeps palming it off. I don't want therapy—a lot of fucking good that did Kelly. And I couldn't care less if I upset a bunch of Year 7 students. I am upset. That was the whole point.

The strategy they came up with was for me to go back to doing a shortened timetable for a few weeks. Mrs Bryan told us she was concerned about how much school I'd missed and even suggested that I might have to repeat. Dad wasn't aware of how much school I'd actually missed because I keep wagging and coming to work instead.

I used to do okay at school. Bs and Cs in most of my

subjects. I don't love any of them though, and I have no idea what I want to do when I leave. No idea. Not like Kel. She had it all mapped out.

'I'll give myself ten months to save and then I'll leave in October on my birthday. There's no point going until we're eighteen anyway.' Kelly looked at me, flicking through a magazine sitting on my bedroom floor, her long dark ponytail swishing.

'I'll be away for at least five years and I'll tick off all of Europe. I'll meet some cute English guy and fall crazy in love and then he'll come back here with me and we'll buy a Transit van and travel around the whole of Australia. He'll then, like, propose to me at Ayers Rock and we'll get married and like have a million babies and how funny is it going to be when we're mums?'

I laughed at her and scrunched my nose. 'Some cute English guy?'

'He'll be my best souvenir, plus Aussie guys are so gross. I can't wait to see the Eiffel Tower and I want to do that tomato festival in Spain and run with the bulls. Girls aren't meant to do it, but fuck that,' she said, jumping to her knees and leaning on the edge of the bed, 'and I want to go to Amsterdam. It's legal to get stoned there, Aves, like on the street, and there's no cars, just bicycles. And you'll be there.'

'For five years?' I laugh.

'I'm not going on my own. Besides, what else are you going to do?' She nudged my leg with her hands so I'd scoot over and we'd both fit. 'Come, Aves. We can meet brothers and we won't get a Transit van, we'll get an old bus and we'll transform it. Can you imagine?'

'We would have the best time.' I laughed, thinking about all the sorts of crazy shit we would get up to.

'We could have a double wedding.' She grabbed my hands, looking like she was about to explode with excitement. 'Would you have a double wedding?'

'With you?' I squealed. 'Oh my god! We can walk down the aisle together with our dads.' I stared at her, mouth wide.

'Holy shit, Aves,' Kelly shrieked, 'our life is going to be so amazing.'

Our life is going to be so amazing. Right.

I'm completely in my own world when Ricky yells from the back of the shop, 'There's a new dishie starting tonight. Help him out.' He steps to the side and standing next to him is a tall, skinny guy with curly hair that covers his forehead but it's short at the back and sides. He's got one arm wrapped around his elbow and he's biting his lip. He looks nervous. I roll my eyes at Ricky.

'*This is Gideon!*' Ricky shouts, and the new guy turns and looks at me then immediately looks away. Dishwashers at Magic Kebab never last because it's the shittest job ever. They all realise within a couple of weeks that washing up salad dishes and crusty meat trays and hosing out manky drains is nothing like the easy and luxurious position that Ricky led them to believe it would be, and they quit. All of them. As I make my way out the back I wonder how long this guy will last. I'm going to guess not very long by the looks of him.

GIDEON

'You're new.' A girl appears and slams a bright purple apron into my chest. When I finally have a chance to register her face I realise I know who she is.

I swallow. 'Yes.' I'm feeling nervous in the way that new things and pretty girls combined make me feel. I start sweating.

'Welcome to Magic Kebab.' She looks at me and I stare at her and in my head I'm screaming at myself to be normal and not to be weird and to say something funny, but all that comes out is 'Thank you?'

After my last session with Robbie he made a phone call to a friend of his, Ricky, who owns Magic Kebab, and asked if he needed any help. It turned out he did and I was told to drop in and have a chat, which turned out to be more like a short encounter than a chat.

'What's your name, Skinny?' Ricky asked as soon

as I'd walked into the shop.

'Gideon.'

'Gideon? Okay. Your job would be to wash up, sweep, maybe cut some tomatoes. No serving. All out the back. Good?' Ricky turned around and went back to shaving a big doner kebab.

'Yeah.'

'You can wash up, yeah?'

'Yes. Yup.'

'Good. Come on Thursday afternoon. Wear old clothes. Good? Good.' And he walked out the back and left me standing there on my own. I wouldn't have got so worked up about the other job interview if I knew that's how easy they were.

'What school do you go to?' she asks.

'Yours,' and she raises her eyebrows at me. Great first impression, Gideon, you look like a stalker.

'What grade?'

'Twelve.'

'Are you new there too?' she asks. Excellent. She has absolutely no idea who I am. Why would she, though? I have no idea who I am. I don't know why Ava Spirini would have any idea who I am.

'I came in Year 9.' I follow her as she walks a few steps and waits for me at the cold-room door.

'That's not new. What's your name?'

'Gideon.'

'Where is that from?' She wrenches the big silver latch on the door and forces it open and I just stand watching her. She's really pretty. Like really, really. She has wild sun-kissed brown hair that twists and curls and sits on her shoulders, but with this blunt fringe that just makes her dark eyebrows and big, big brown eyes stand out more. She has olive skin and broad shoulders and she's short. She only comes up to my chest.

'A musical,' I say.

'Really?'

'And the Bible,' I mutter and wish I hadn't.

'What's it about?'

'Well, there's this guy named Jesus and he—'

'No, the musical.' She smirks just a little. I know because I watch the corner of her mouth ever so slightly twitch. It only lasts a couple of seconds but I know it happened. I know it happened because my gut kind of tensed when it did. While I'm busy thinking about the feeling in my stomach my mouth starts a ramble that I have absolutely no control of.

'It's about these seven lumberjack brothers who live in the mountains who kidnap seven women and they cause this big avalanche so that the women can't be rescued'—I pause, very briefly thinking that I'm finished, but no, my mouth has other ideas—'then they spend the winter making the girls fall in love with them.'

'How?'

'What?'

'How do they make the girls fall in love with them?' Ava steps onto a small ladder to get something down off the top shelf and her T-shirt lifts up a bit, revealing her back, the waistband of her denim shorts and her undies. They're blue. I close my eyes and quickly look away. *Come on Gideon, get your shit together.* Don't be the creeper who loses it at the sight of real-life girl flesh and knowing personal details about them like the colour of their underwear.

'Um. Snowball fights and flowers and they injure themselves so the girls feel sorry for them,' I blurt. Ava makes a sound. I don't want to call it a laugh, because I don't think that's what it was. It was more of a breathy sound out of her nose with the same smirk. She steps off the ladder and hands me a two-kilo tin of dolmades.

'Oh, they sing, there's singing too,' I add and then there's a silence.

Ava bends down to get something from the bottom shelf of the fridge.

'That synopsis didn't really do it justice,' I mumble.

If ever there was time for a pep talk it is now. Every internal part of me that has had something to do with this abysmal attempt at conversation is now scolding the other parts of me that stood by and let it happen. *What are you doing, man?* they scream, *get it together!* I should be used to this by now though, my general flailing demeanour when it comes to conversation, because I'm just not good at it. I get nervous then I don't know what to say or I say too much or say something stupid. And I never know what to do with my hands. If you add to this the extra level of excruciating rambling that happens because Ava Spirini is a girl my age then I'm basically the coolest guy ever.

I'm this shit around everyone, though, not just Ava.

All human people. All the time. My brain has this habit of convincing me that everyone thinks I'm a hideous human who can do nothing right. Robbie repeatedly tells me this isn't the case and how dare I be so narcissistic as to think people would give up worrying about their own crippling insecurities to devote any time to analysing mine.

'It really didn't.' Ava stands and hands me a large plastic bowl filled with lettuce. I weigh up the pros and cons of just walking out the door with the lettuce and the tin of dolmades and never returning.

'I've never met a Gideon,' she says as she shuts the big fridge door.

'I've never met an Ava.' I smile and she smiles, and the biggest wave of relief washes over me because for someone with my track record, that wasn't too bad. I didn't look like too much of an idiot.

For the rest of the night, aside from her firing instructions like 'Fill that' or 'Wash this' or 'Get me that' we don't talk.

I wash dishes until my hands go pruney and as I wash I watch Ava Spirini's back and I think as far as jobs go this one seems to be okay.

I was probably one of the last people to find out about her friend, Kelly. Kelly Waititi. Kelly was beautiful. No, beautiful isn't right. She was breathtaking. She had long jet-black hair and massive brown eyes and dark brown skin. I think she must've been Maori or Islander or something. She didn't give a shit about anything. My locker was right near hers and this one time I was going home early for a doctor's appointment or something, and while I was getting my bag she walked in, opened her locker and just started getting changed. She didn't say anything, just stood there in her bra while she rifled around her bag for her dress, put it on, flung her bag over her shoulder and went to leave. Just before she got to the door she turned back to me, and asked, 'Are you wagging too?' I shook my head; she nodded and walked out.

That's the only time that Kelly ever spoke directly to me, but I knew who she was. Everyone knew who she was, and I guess purely by association if you knew who Kelly was you knew who Ava was because they were always together. From what I know about Ava, she's fiery but quiet and funny; everyone is always cracking up when they're around her. Or at least they were. Lately when I see her at school she's always on her own. I think she's pretty. Like, really pretty. Noticeable; or at least I always notice her. At assembly last week she yelled at the top of her lungs for everyone to get fucked, and still managed to crack jokes as she stormed out the hall giving Mrs Bryan the finger.

I can't imagine how she feels. No one I love has ever died. I still have four grandparents and the same dog I've had since I was five. The only person I know who was even close to dying is me. And that wouldn't have been devastating at all; that would've been a giant relief. Or at least I thought it would've been at the time.

•

'Right. Check in, Gideon, what number are you?' Ria says. Ria is mad and curvy; her head is shaved really short except for a middle section at the top which drapes down the side of her face that she dyes different colours. At the moment her hair is silver-grey, like if your nanna was a hipster. Ria is covered in tattoos, small ones intricately placed all over her body and she has a Doctor Who–themed sleeve that runs down her whole left arm. Ria and Robbie are friends. Robbie is how I met Ria three years ago and started doing classes, then poetry competitions, then hanging out with a group of about fifteen kids my age writing, making theatre and short films and stuff. At first it was about confidence and, as Robbie would put it, 'normal social interactions with peers'. But there is nothing definitively normal about the peers that I now hang out with.

'I'm a seven,' I say and the group nod and smile. Ria operates the beginning of every workshop like this, with a number system that runs between one and ten. One meaning that it's the worst day of your life and you couldn't possibly feel any worse. When I started classes with Ria I was a two, maybe three at best. I took the scale seriously, unlike some of the other people in the group who would be a one when they had a pimple or their parents wouldn't buy them a skinny latte on the way to class. But that's why it's a number scale and not a whiney monologue scale: everyone can understand numbers. Who's to say my two was different to their two? Maybe they really, really wanted a coffee. Maybe there was a promise involved, or the love of their life was the barista they'd promised to visit that afternoon and their villainous parent saying no to the coffee meant that the barista hopped on a plane to Nepal never knowing how they felt. Or something.

'Seven? Good. And question?' Ria smiles at me. She has a small plastic ball in her hand that she's throwing up in the air as she speaks and she's wearing a bracelet that jingles when she does it. There's a new question every week—they vary in levels of seriousness. Sometimes we spend hours talking existentially about our purpose in the world, other times we discuss who'd die first if there was a zombie attack. This week's question is: *If you could have any superpower in the world what would it be?*

'Invisibility,' I say.

'Bullshit,' Norma yells across the room.

'Seconded,' Andy, who sits next to me, chimes in with lightning speed, slapping me hard on the leg.

'Why?' Norma sits cross-legged with her eyebrows raised at me, her tight auburn ringlets springing from her head like a wild mane.

'It's true,' I say. I'm used to this from Norma and Andy, they're my closest friends. I met them in a circle similar to this in my first class years ago. 'Because, imagine being able to become invisible. You could listen to people's conversations or whisper things in their ear or move their shit around. I think it would be hilarious.' I smile, a few of the other kids laugh and come up with their ideas about being in the boys' locker room after sport or pulling the chair out from underneath their most hated teacher.

'You already make yourself invisible, Gids,' Norma shouts across the circle.

'Okay, okay,' Ria says, her group of unruly teenagers suddenly becoming more and more out of control. 'Gideon do you want to respond to that comment?'

'Nope.' I shake my head and give Norma the finger.

Andy leans in and whispers, 'Norma's such a bitch,' then laughs his weird high-pitched giggle that makes him sound like one of the hyenas in *The Lion King*.

Andy was the first person to talk to me on my first day. Just strolled over in a tie-dye T-shirt, all moving limbs and swirls of colour, and said, 'Are you gay?' before he even asked my name.

'No.'

'Me neither. Be careful.'

'What?'

'Of the girls. They're like vultures.'

'What?'

'They mostly go to all-girls schools and the only guys they know are gay. You're handsome. They'll like you.'

'Oh. Okay.' The only people who'd ever called me handsome before Andy were my mums.

'Do you have a girlfriend?'

'No.'

'Cool. Then take your pick.' He signalled around the room. 'Except Norma, I like Norma. And not Bridie.'

'Why not Bridie?' I ask.

'Because she's a bitch.'

Andy and I became immediate allies and then friends. Norma and Andy got together right after that, and thus have been a couple for as long as I've known them. You know those couples that are creepily kind of destined for each other? At fourteen, that can only mean they're bound to fail. Except for the rare exception.

Andy and Norma are that rare exception.

Class proceeds and we discuss important topics like what Sally should do with her hair, if Travis should break up with his boyfriend and the podcast we've all been listening to.

I like coming here. It's like exhaling amid an existence of holding your breath. There's no pressure or bullshit. The only expectations are that you're honest and considerate of others, you give everything a go and you don't act like a dick. I think the world could learn a lot from Ria and how she runs her class.

This week they lay a heap of different pictures on the ground and we have to use them as stimulus to write something. I take a picture of a trampoline and write a poem about a girl lying underneath a trampoline, feeling the adrenaline as her friend jumps on it above her. Issy has to read it out loud and does a great job. Issy has a pixie cut and phenomenally long eyelashes. She is equal measures confident and self-deprecating, and the worst part of having no internet at the moment is not being able to chat to her. Just stupid conversations where we'd send shit memes to each other, but still.

'I hope that was okay,' she says as she sits down, and I nod.

It was. She was. She's a really good performer. 'I think I fucked it,' she goes on.

'Yup. Totally. I'm glad you said something because you were really shit actually,' I crack, shaking my head.

'Shut up.' She whacks me on the shoulder and turns away just as I catch Norma and Andy looking at me with raised eyebrows and Andy mouths: *You're in.*

'She was so flirting with you,' Norma says as we stand around outside waiting for our parents to pick us up.

'Piss off.'

'She was. Wasn't she, babe?'

'There was a definite aroma of flirtation in the air,' Andy smiles.

'That's disgusting,' I say, shaking my head.

'Do you like her?' Norma asks.

'She's nice.'

'Yeah, but do you want to make out with her face?'

'What other part are you meant to make out with?'

Andy shakes his head, disappointed. 'So much to learn, my friend.'

'I think you're in with a definite chance,' Norma nods.

'I'll think about it,' I reply.

Think about it? It's probably all I'll think about now that Norma has planted the seed. Do I like Issy?

I've never thought about it. Not really. We get along, but it's not like there's some unavoidable chemistry or anything. But then I would have no idea if there was anyway, because I have almost zero experience when it comes to girls.

I have kissed two, Stacey Knight and Rebecca Simons. On the same night. Within five minutes of each other. I was in Year 9 and we were in Andy's garage. I had just joined Ria's class and Andy had what he called a 'gathering'. It was the first thing I'd ever been invited to that I'd agreed to attend.

There were only about ten people there and we were playing a game of 'prison rules' Uno, which is basically where you assign actions to the numbers. Like if you're the last two people to place your hands on your head when a red eight is placed on the pile, you have to kiss.

WHAT I THOUGHT WHEN I KISSED STACEY KNIGHT (IN ORDER OF APPEARANCE IN MY BRAIN)

1. I can actually feel her tongue in my mouth.
2. This is disgusting.
3. Slugs.
4. How do I get her to stop licking my chin?
5. This is incredibly disappointing.
6. Don't act disappointed. This could entirely be your fault. What if you're a crap kisser and you made this happen?

WHAT I THOUGHT WHEN I KISSED REBECCA
SIMONS (IN ORDER OF APPEARANCE IN MY BRAIN)

1. Oh. Okay. This is different.
2. This is better.
3. THIS IS THE BEST THING IN THE WHOLE FREAKING WORLD.
4. Why aren't people just making out all of the time? Because it would be completely understandable.
5. Phew. It's not my fault. Either that or I am an incredibly quick learner.

I have not kissed anyone else since. The opportunity has not arisen, mainly because of my deep-seated fear of, well, everyone. And when you add crippling fear to a propensity for anxiety and panic attacks, you know what that equals?

Fear + panic attacks + generally anxious persona = Gideon's failure as a social being.

I am a slow burn. Like a really slow burn. It takes me a very long time to feel comfortable enough to not freak out. Which is why my sister is my best mate, why I have no friends at school and why the idea of Issy liking me is making the muscles in my throat constrict so I'm finding it kind of hard to breathe.

•

I've never been drunk. Ever. And now that I've done four full weekend shifts at Magic Kebab and seen a throng of intoxicated people falling over themselves, yelling ridiculous things and spewing in bins outside the shop, I can't see the appeal. Last Saturday there was a stupid drunk girl wearing a flower crown and holding her shoes who'd been crying so much her cheeks were eighty-five per cent mascara and she yelled at Ava over and over again that she was 'a fucking pescatarian' and that she could only eat chicken. Ava tried to tell her what a pescatarian is but the girl just cried louder and ended up throwing one of her heels over the counter at Ava, yelling, 'I just want a chicken kebab.' One of her friends had to grab her and pull her away and I couldn't help it, I started giggling as I was filling up the tomatoes. Ava just rolled her eyes at me and mouthed the word, *Watch*. She quickly filled the girl's kebab with Ricky's chilli sauce and burnt bits of lamb, then walked around the counter and handed the kebab to the girl with a curtsy. The girl just rolled her eyes and scoffed down half of the kebab before dropping the other half all over her boobs. By which point Ava and I were slumped behind the counter laughing.

'What an idiot,' she said, tucking her wild brown hair behind her ear. And I just smiled and said nothing, because that's what I do.

The three shifts before that she hadn't said anything to me apart from 'We need more onions,' and 'Be careful with the olives, you'll get a rash.' I did get a rash and I had to get Mum to come and pick me up.

Thursday nights are better. Quieter. More opportunities for talking. For banter. I have a pre-prepared list of appropriate or possible topics for attempting to banter with Ava tonight, because I figure if I just keep nodding and smiling when she talks to me she's going to start to think that I'm a complete doofus, or more of a doofus than she no doubt already does.

APPROPRIATE OR POSSIBLE BANTERING TOPICS

1. Movies

2. Music.

3. TV.

4. Something funny that happens at the shop.

5. The weather.

I ask Susan for help in the car on the way to work.

'Do not under any circumstances talk about the weather,' Susan sighs.

'Okay,' I reply.

'And do not make a list.'

'I'm not,' I tell her as the list in my pocket burns a metaphorical hole in my leg.

'Just ask her questions. And don't be weird,' she says as she checks the rearview mirror.

'Yeah, easier said than done,' I scoff.

'Take the pressure off. You just want to talk to her, you don't want to sleep with her.' She smiles, knowing I'll freak out.

'*Susan,*' I freak out.

She quickly cuts me off. 'Unless you do and that's fine too. Like mother like son,' she says with her deep raspy giggle.

'You are disgusting. You have been with the same

woman for twenty-five years, you don't know shit.'

'Back in the day I was a force to be reckoned with.'

'I do not want to be a force or anything else. I just...'
I pause. What do I want? 'I just want her to not think
I'm an idiot.'

'You're not an idiot, my boy. You're the smartest
person I know.' She pats my leg. 'Just be natural and
stop thinking about it. Which I know for you is like
telling the Pope to stop being Catholic, but you get what
I mean.'

When I walk into the shop I throw the list in the bin and
count to thirty before I go back and retrieve it and put
it in my pocket. Just in case. It doesn't matter, though.
Ava only says one word to me.

'Hey.'

'Hey!' I reply. So far, so good.

Later in the night Ricky puts on another one of his
records and whacks me on the back. 'I bet you don't
know who this is, Skinny.'

'It's Led Zeppelin,' I say as Ricky dances around
me.

'Ava didn't know who it was, did you Ava?'

She looks up at us. 'Nope. Time for an iPod, Ricky.'

'Bullshit. I don't want that digital crap. Records are
better.'

'I kind of collect records,' I mutter.

Ricky laughs loudly. 'See?' His whole belly moving.
'You *kind of* collect records?' Ava looks at me.

'I do,' I say. 'Collect them.'

Ava nods and walks off. I guess that kind of counts as banter, doesn't it?

I take a moment with my elbows deep in greasy water to pat myself on the back for the two relatively normal interactions I've managed this evening.

Later a group of young African guys are sitting at the corner table beatboxing and freestyling lyrics, every now and then cheering or cracking up, pointing at the one who was just rapping. I eavesdrop as I empty the bins and realise that the majority of the reaction comes when they say stupid shit about each other's mums. When I walk back into the shop after taking the rubbish bags to the big industrial bin outside, the shop is empty apart from their table and one of the boys calls me over. I look over at Ava for a second. She's standing behind the counter, just kind of smirking as the four boys start hassling me to join in with them.

'You do a verse. You do a verse,' the one with the hat asks.

'No. I couldn't,' I say. 'Thank you for asking, though,' and they laugh at me. The smallest guy, who is wearing a zebra-print button-up shirt, puts his arm around my shoulder and ushers me back to their table.

'You can. You can,' he says.

'I can't. I dunno what...' I stutter, but the boys just yell that yeah I can, and to say the first thing that comes to mind.

'No pressure,' says a guy with the biggest smile I've ever seen in my life. They start banging on the table and cheering, one of them freestyles a bit, then the next guy takes his turn and then all at once they look at me and the guy beatboxing continues. My cheeks flush as they all stare at me, waiting for me to do something. Anything. I can literally feel the pump of adrenaline course through my body. I take a second to thank Ria for the hundreds of improvisation games and freestyle writing prompts she's made me do over the years.

And I open my mouth.

> I don't know what you want me to do, in fact I kinda feel sick. / I don't wanna be rude about your mums, cause that's kinda misogynistic. / If they heard the way you rapped about them I think they'd get a fright, / But don't worry boys I'll make them feel better, when I'm in bed with them tonight.

AVA

I'm shocked. Like dead-set floored. My mouth is gaping, my eyes wide and my eyebrows wilder. The four African boys erupt, jumping in the air shouting and laughing as one of them picks up Gideon over his shoulders hugging him and the others pat him on the head.

'That was sick, yeah?' one of the boys yells over to me.

'Yeah,' I say. *Who the fuck is this guy?* He's all shy and nervous and barely says a word and then he turns out to be some random MC. I giggle as I watch them and it quickly turns to fully blown, gut-tensing laughter as I watch Gideon get thrown around by the boys patting him on the back.

I listen to them talk about music they all like and hip-hop artists they all know and eventually the boys come back to earth shaking their heads in disbelief, saying things like, 'Boy, you smooth,' and 'Yes! Yes!'

Gideon just grins, awkward, his cheeks bright red as the boys walk out of the shop, completely impressed. Then he turns on his heel, looks at the floor and walks straight past the counter. Two seconds later he appears with a broom and starts to sweep.

'You're not going to say anything about what just happened?' I ask, and he shakes his head. 'What? You're just like secretly Shakespeare over there with the broom?'

'Nah, nah,' he mutters.

'Bullshit,' I say.

'I write.'

'You write?'

'Yeah. Poems,' he says.

'Cool.'

'Yeah?' he asks. He's looking at me properly for the first time.

'That was cool,' I say, smiling, because it was.

'Yeah?' he asks again, and I nod.

I think he's cute, in a nerdy hipster kind of way, only he's not a hipster because his hair is too messy and his clothes are way too big.

Once the shop is closed and we've packed everything up Gideon and I wait out the front. I don't know why, but the words that come out of my mouth next don't actually feel like my own.

'You should ask me for my number,' I say as I fumble around my backpack for the last cigarette I stole from Lincoln.

Gideon is dumbfounded, he kind of stutters his answer. 'I, I, I should?'

'Yes.'

'I should. But—' He stops himself.

But? But what? He has a girlfriend? I don't think he has a girlfriend. He thinks I'm hitting on him. Am I hitting on him? I don't think I'm hitting on him. I'm definitely not hitting on him. Do I need to make it really obvious to him that I am definitely not hitting on him? I don't know what I'm doing. I think he's funny. I like the way I feel when I'm around him. I'm curious.

'But?' I ask. I finally find the cigarette among all the other shit in my bag and begin the hunt for a lighter.

'I don't have a phone,' he says and I don't even bother to look up because I know he's joking and he'll tell me the real reason soon. Like, he thinks I'm too fucked up or he's moving to Botswana to work in a commune and he won't get reception so there's no point.

Gideon doesn't say anything. I look at him. Holy shit. He's serious.

'Really?'

'Yeah.'

'Well. You should add me,' I say.

'I don't have the internet either,' he says with a smile and a deep breath out. He jams his hands in his pockets and looks at the ground.

'Really?'

'Yes. Really.' Gideon doesn't look up, he keeps looking at the ground, making patterns in the dirt. His curls bounce with each movement of his foot. He's tall. Taller than me, taller than Lincoln even. And he's skinny. Not like you can see his ribs skinny, but still skinny. His jeans are like super tight and they're tucked into these shiny black boots and his long-sleeve shirt is probably five sizes too big. It suits him, though. He doesn't look like anyone I know. If anything he looks like the long-haired retro musos on the cover of Ricky's vinyls.

Gideon doesn't say anything. So I don't say anything. No phone and no internet. Maybe he is actually from the seventies and I'm in some weird time parallel universe thing. Great, that's all I need this year, to become friends with some time-travelling guy. I have to smile at that.

'If you don't want to talk to me you can just say no,' I finally say, and I start the search for the lighter again.

'No—'

'Oh!' I take two steps back. Wow.

At least he was honest. He doesn't want to talk to me, and who can blame him? I mean I *am* pretty fucked up at the moment and it doesn't take a detective to work that out.

'No, I mean, no I do want to talk to you—'

''Cause that's fine. I just thought that...' I kind of mutter. Actually I don't know what I thought. Or why I even asked in the first place. I don't even care.

Only I do, because I have that feeling in my stomach, that rejected feeling, the one that I swear every time I put myself in a stupid situation like this that I'm never, ever going to do ever again because it's too embarrassing.

When I'd try and tell Kel about this feeling she'd shrug and tell me I was an idiot, tell me she had no idea what I meant. And she didn't because no one rejected Kelly. Not boys. Not girls. Not teachers. No one. Only Kelly's brain rejected Kelly.

Gideon takes two steps towards me. 'Ava? I really, actually, like swear on both my mothers' lives that I don't have a phone.'

'Or the internet?'

'Or the internet.'

'A house phone?' I ask.

'Who has a house phone anymore? Um. No,' he says, trying to lighten the mood.

'We do,' I say.

'Oh,' Gideon fumbles. I don't know why we still have a house phone. It's only telemarketers and my Yiayia who ever call it.

There's a silence. An awkward silence. I feel around in my bag again for the lighter and find it in the front pocket. Finally. I light it and take a deep drag.

'How come?' I ask.

'I thought I'd see what life was like without them,' he says, nodding, with his hands in his pockets.

I take another drag. 'How is life without them?' I offer the cigarette to Gideon and he shakes his head.

'I'm still deciding.'

I'm intrigued. What would make anyone in their right mind want to know what life was like without a phone and the internet? Gideon is nervous around me. I like that about him. People are never nervous around me. I'm nervous around them. Around everyone, but not Gideon. I wonder if there's some kind of quota between two people where there can only be so many nerves, and because Gideon fills the quota between us I don't have to feel them. I don't feel much lately, apart from really angry or kind of numb, but around Gideon I feel this sense of...control, almost. Not like I'm controlling him, but confidence, like I'm in charge because he's so nervous.

I wonder if this is how Kel used to feel. She'd flick her long hair back over her head, roll her neck back and shake out her shoulders like one of those girls in a Bond movie. She'd drag long and hard on her cigarettes and tie her T-shirts in knots above her belly button. Kelly didn't give a fuck. When she decided she liked Faye Donaldson it was on. Even though Faye Donaldson had never kissed a girl. In actual fact, I don't think Faye Donaldson had ever kissed anyone.

'She's beautiful, Aves. I don't think anyone has ever told her she's beautiful,' Kelly said.

'Her mum, probably,' I told her.

'That doesn't count.' She'd stubbed out her cigarette on the ground and took her iPod out of her pocket. I was sitting on the ground on the edge of the oval at the back entrance to the school. Kels held out her hand to me and I took it, and she pulled me up. Looked me right in the eye.

'Imagine going your whole life without anyone telling you you're beautiful.'

'What are you going to do?'

'I'm going to tell her.' Kel placed the ear buds in my ears and hit play and I stood watching her as she walked over to Faye Donaldson, who was just waiting, unsuspecting. I watched Kelly talk to her for a bit. I watched Faye smile and reply. Then Kelly must have told her she was beautiful because Faye blushed and looked away. Kel closed the gap between them, tucked Faye's hair behind her ear and then she kissed her with both hands on her cheeks. Sweet, slow, lovely. Not for very long, but long enough. Finally Kelly pulled away and kissed her on the cheek and smiled, and then started the walk back to me. All the while some acoustic ballad blaring in my ears and me feeling like I was watching a movie, some high school romance, play out in front of me. I shook my head as Kel smiled and hooked her arm through mine. She took one earpiece from me and put it in her ear as we walked off together.

Faye came to the funeral. Or at least the service part of the funeral. Kelly had a traditional Maori funeral. Or as traditional as they could make it without actually being in New Zealand. They set up a marae in their lounge room where the coffin lay open for two days, and on the third day we had the actual service. They wanted it to be at the house but too many people were going to come so they had it in this big church hall. During the two days people came and visited and saw her and she was never left on her own. I slept in the room with them all on the second night, and by sleep I mean lay staring at the ceiling or holding Lincoln's hand.

I was the only kid from school who went to the house. I think people were freaked out about seeing her in her coffin. I don't blame them. I was so scared of seeing her. I didn't know what to expect. I wasn't sure if I'd cope, and the last thing I wanted was to upset everyone even more. But Dad came with me and as I sat on the couch taking it all in, Dad sat with Kelly's dad, Greg, next to the coffin and they both cried. Dad whispered something to Kelly as he kissed her forehead and big fat tears dropped from his eyes. Tina looked at me and gestured for me to come over. I remember this nauseous kind of feeling rising up from my toes to the tip of my head and then back down again. I nodded and cried and sat next to her and she put her arm around me as I looked at my friend.

Kelly didn't look like herself. Her brown, brown skin was greyish now and she was so, so still.

Over the two days Kelly's family sat around and played guitar and cried and talked to her. I found it so hard to say anything with everyone around but I'd steal little moments where I'd just hold her hand and I'd try and will my brain to understand that she was actually gone.

At sunrise on the third day there was a ceremony where Kelly's aunties sang songs and people said prayers and they put the lid on the coffin. I will never ever for as long as I live forget the sounds Tina made as she sat hugging the coffin. It was more than a cry, it was a howl. More animal than human. Sometimes when it's really quiet I'm positive I can still hear it, as though it's burnt into my soul. That's what pain sounds like. We watched as they put the coffin in the car; I think that was the worst part. I couldn't stop my tears, and my legs folded underneath me so Dad stood behind me with his arms around my waist, holding me up, and then the hearse drove away and I would never see my beautiful friend again.

Heaps of people from school came to the funeral. Heaps of kids that made no sense were there. There were girls who hated Kelly standing there crying and I remember so desperately wanting to tell them to get fucked. But I didn't. I stood with Dad and felt like a heavy zombie. I didn't say anything to anyone except Faye Donaldson, who came up to me.

'I'm so sorry, Ava.' She was looking at the ground.

'She meant it, yeah?' I told her.

'What?'

'She thought you were beautiful.'

Faye took a big shaky breath in and she squeezed my hand, nodded, and walked off.

I draw back on the cigarette and look at Gideon. 'So what do you do if you meet a girl?'

'I don't.'

'What?'

'Meet girls. I didn't think. I don't have a plan.' He takes his hands out of his pockets and they move about wildly as he talks. They match the energy in his words, like they're dancing and his words are the music. I'm kind of mesmerised by it and I want him to keep talking.

'How do you talk to anyone?'

'I don't.' He shakes his head and his hands fly up like they don't know either and then they hit his thighs and make a clapping sound. I throw the cigarette on the ground and stand on it.

'Really?'

'Well, I do. My family. But. They live in my house so—'

I cut him off. '...It's easy.'

'Yeah.' He kind of half-chuckles, so I half-laugh too, but it's mostly air, not a real laugh. Kel reckons you always know what I'm thinking because it's on my face. I'm not a good liar. I think it's my eyebrows—they kind of have a life of their own. I blame my Pappou for my Greek eyebrows; they're his eyebrows.

'Do you at least have a TV?'

'Yeahhhhh,' Gideon says, like I'm an idiot.

'Phew,' I grin. 'I was beginning to think you were *really* weird.'

Gideon laughs, nervous but genuine, and I smile and bite my lip and wonder how I've never met him before.

'So now what?' I ask. A four-wheel drive pulls up just near us and beeps its horn.

'That's my mum.' Gideon smiles. 'Do you need a lift?'

'No.'

'Okay.' He nods and takes two steps away before pivoting around on the toes of one foot. 'School? I can see you at school.'

'I don't really. I'm not really. I don't know about—' I stop.

'After all the stuff?' he says. Of course he knows about 'all the stuff'. Probably saw my performance at assembly and knows about Kel. That's why he's being so nice to me, doesn't want to send me off the rails. The car beeps its horn again, he takes two quick strides towards it and waves, holding up five fingers and then a thumbs-up.

But when he comes back the feeling from before is gone. I don't need Gideon's sympathy. I don't need anyone's sympathy. What I need is my mate back. That's what I need.

'Okay. Um. A letter.' Gideon is bouncing and catches me off guard.

'What?'

'I'll write you a letter. What's your address?'

'Really?'

'Yeah, and then you can reply. If you want. And I'll see you here. At work.' He's talking really fast, looking at me, rubbing his hands together. I'm perplexed and perplexed is what is all over my face. My eyebrows are having a field day with this guy.

'Are you even?' I laugh. 'Are you even real?'

'Yes. What's your address?'

I reach inside my bag, take my payslip and rip off the corner with my address on it and hand it to him. He clutches it and holds it in his hand.

'Good. Cool.' He smiles, still bouncing.

'Cool.'

'Letters,' he says, pacing two steps away from me, then turning back again. 'Goodnight Ava.'

And he walks away, gets in the car and goes. I watch until the headlights on his car become tiny yellow specks and I do something I feel like I haven't done in a very long time. I breathe. A long, hard, loud exhale out of my mouth, and I smile. Not because of Gideon, though; because of something else, because of how I feel. Normal.

•

'Ava, I want you to tell me in your own words what you think happened today,' Mrs Bryan says, staring at me from across her desk while my dad puts his hand on my shoulder and I close my eyes and breathe through my nose.

'Trevor Lane called her a psycho bitch,' I say.

'Called who?'

'Who do you think?'

'Ava.' My dad stops me and squeezes my shoulder.

I'm furious. My knuckles are bleeding, my stomach muscles hurt and my throat is on fire from scream-ing. If Mr Barnaby hadn't pulled me away and liter-ally carried me down to the office as I punched and screamed and hurled my body around I would've surely killed Trevor. I'd overheard him whispering about me, about her under his breath. Saying he was glad she died. As I explain this to Mrs Bryan, she cuts me off. 'Now Ava, I'm sure that Trevor didn't—'

'He said it. He meant it. He's a fucking idiot.'

'Oi, kiddo, check your manners,' Dad mumbles. The blinds cast long line shadows onto his forehead and it makes his furrow look even more intense.

'Sorry.' I look at Mrs Bryan. 'Sorry. I'm just—angry. It made me angry.'

'So what happened?'

'I told him to shut his mouth.'

'While Mr Barnaby was teaching?'

'Yes.'

'And then?'

And then the slimy douchebag that is Trevor Lane looked at me with his greasy skin and eyes so dark they look black and sneered: 'I wish you were the one who'd topped herself. At least the other one was hot.'

My blood turned to molten lava and lifted my feet off the ground with such force that my fist connected with his face. The punch knocked him back onto the floor as I scrambled over the desk to hit him again. And again. It was around this time that Mr Barnaby lifted me under my arms and carried me out of the room.

'You didn't mean to hit him though, Ava?' Mrs Bryan asks.

'I did.'

'But you were angry and sometimes when we're angry we—' I can't believe she's trying to pretend like it didn't happen. This has been the main problem this whole time, everyone palming shit off like it's no big deal.

'I meant it. I did it on purpose. I think he's vile. I'm not sorry. And I won't apologise to him. I'd do it again.' I look across at my dad, who shifts his chin slightly but I can see that he's smirking.

'Oh. Um. Well. In that case, Ava. You know that we have zero tolerance for any kind of physical violence.'

'What about Trevor?' I ask.

'What about him?'

'What he said.'

'I will speak to Trevor.'

'But you won't punish him.' I shake my head.

'We will take the necessary action and make decisions that are specific to his behaviour. I'm sure other kids in the class will vouch for what you've said, Ava?' And I want to punch her now too. She's such a patronising bitch. She thinks this is all my fault. She just hates me because I'm disrupting her day. She doesn't actually give a flying fuck about me.

'Ava, we need to expel you,' she says like it's the easiest thing in the world, like she's just told me what day it is.

'What?' My dad jerks forward and puts his hands on the desk. I don't say anything.

'With your track record this year—'

'I'm sorry, but this is bullshit,' he puffs.

'Dad,' I say; now it's my turn to touch his shoulder.

'You know what she's going through, right?'

'Yes. We understand that Ava has experienced a trauma, we have all experienced a trauma, but I have other students to support. I think we have ceased being able to support Ava here. I think another institution would be best, in fact I've given Rahila Saeed a call at TAPs and she's more than happy to meet with you.'

'At *TAPs*?' I yell, stunned.

'I just think their program is better suited to your specific needs right now, Ava. At least to get you through Year 11 and then you can reassess what your options are at the end of the year. Year 11 is an important foundational year and I don't want you to miss too much.' She slides a bright red and yellow pamphlet over to Dad.

'Her number is on the back.'

She wants me to go to TAPs? TAPs stands for The Alternative Program. It's a bludge school for the teenage mums, the bully victims, the weird kids with too many piercings who all work at Hungry Jack's and the kids with the anger issues who—

Who flip out in class and punch dickheads like Trevor Lane in the nose for saying stupid shit about their friend who died.

'We'll have a look.' Dad stands up. I can tell that he's pissed off; his lips are pursed tightly shut. I follow him to the door.

'I'm sorry we couldn't do more,' Mrs Bryan says, still sitting in her chair as Dad spins, shaking his head and clenching his teeth.

'Well, you haven't really done anything to be honest, Mrs Bryan. In fact I'll be getting in contact with the Department of Education to discuss how poorly MacGreggor College has navigated the death of Kelly, and how unsupportive and ineffective your pastoral care has been.' Dad huffs out a big exhalation of breath and Mrs Bryan just looks dumbfounded. I smile. My dad is awesome.

'Mr Spirini—'

'All the best, Mrs Bryan.' And he puts his arm around my shoulders and walks me to the door, and doesn't say anything till we get to the carpark.

'What a rude, rude woman,' he says as he gets into the car.

'Dad, you were amazing.'

'Just because I'm pissed off with her doesn't mean you're not in trouble. Punching a kid? Jesus, Ava. You can't just go around punching people.'

'I know, but—'

'I know: you were angry, he said shit about Kelly. I get it. But still…' He exhales loudly, stopping himself.

By the time we get home it's been decided that I will be going for a meeting at TAPs. It was Dad who made the decision. I had no say in it at all. I told him I wasn't like those kids at TAPs and he just looked sad and told me I didn't have an option. He lectured me about messing up my education and about being smart and despite Mrs Bryan's capacity to be a right royal bitch she was right about the school's ability to support me and he agreed that maybe TAPs might be a good fit for now. Only Dad didn't call Mrs Bryan a bitch he just called her incompetent.

I feel disappointed with myself, like I've let my dad down, let Kelly down, let myself down. In just a few months everything has changed. I've lost Kelly, everything is shit with her parents and I don't even know what Lincoln and I are doing, I've told the entire school to go fuck themselves, I've punched a guy in the face and now I've been expelled. This morning when I left for school I was naive enough to think that at least things couldn't get worse. I was wrong. I lie on my bed and fume. Things, it would seem, can always be worse.

Dad appears in the doorway and hands me a mint-green envelope. 'Aves, this is for you.' When he's gone I rip it open and inside there's two A4 pages filled with the neatest handwriting I've ever seen.

Hello!

I told you I'd write so I am. It's only as I'm writing this that I realise I don't think I've ever written anyone an actual letter before.

So here goes…

Dear Ava,

I don't know how long letters are meant to be. Do you know? They should be longer than a text message, shouldn't they? And they feel like they should be somewhat more important. But I don't really know anything important to say.

I'm glad we met.

That's important.

So, what do you need to know about me? I'm seventeen. We go to the same school. I'm in Year 12. I have one sister and two mums. I write poems. I like guacamole and I hate bananas—I think they're weird. It's a texture thing, like their hard skin gives off the apparent vibe that they're tougher than they actually are. I hate when you peel them and they're all powdery and way too squishy. Have I just unknowingly come up with an exceptional metaphor for humans? Or am I just wasting your time by talking about bananas to begin with? I don't want to waste your time. In an effort to make you think that I am not in fact weird, here is a list of other things I think are weird. I do not think lists are weird. In fact I like writing lists.

Things Gideon thinks are weird. A list.

1. Bananas—obviously, we just went through this.

2. Snakes. I think it's weird that they can swim but they don't have arms. Did you know that snakes can swim? I didn't either until I watched the movie version of *Tomorrow When the War Began* and there was that whole scene with Fi and the snake in the water. MIND. BLOWN.

3. People who put an 'r' sound in the word ask. No explanation needed.

4. People who are able to write letters that do not include lists. Okay this is a lie and a quite obvious effort to make myself look cooler than I actually am. Which I'm assuming you've worked out by now is not very cool at all.

5. People who are naturally and effortlessly cool. Which, I'm sorry to have to say, Ava Spirini, is you. I don't know if that's appropriate letter etiquette to call the recipient of your letter weird. But, there you go: rules are meant to be broken, right?

So, write back. If you, you know, want to. I hope you do.

From

Gideon

It's brilliant. It's perfectly dorky and smart and cool and funny all at once. I never for a second thought he'd really write me a letter, especially not one that revealed actual information about himself. I read the letter again. Gideon is funny. I feel completely confused by him, like I've never met anyone like him. I don't know what I'd say if I wrote back. I should probably write back.

Yeah. I wouldn't want him to think that I didn't want to be his friend.

GIDEON

Tonight's competition is in a coffee shop in the middle of town. There's about thirty people huddled around small tables or sitting on small couches and cushions. Norma and Andy and some other kids from my drama group are sitting right at the front. Mum and Susan are standing at the back. Mum has her glasses on and is taking about a million photos. The two of them spend a good five minutes trying to work out how to switch it to video so they can email it to Annie when we get home.

When it's my turn I inhale deep and take a step towards the microphone.

'This is called "Broken",' I say.

when i was nine i broke my ankle; / a scooter slide into a concrete drive will do that / the doctor, a lady, i noticed her eyes, / the blue of satellite skies, / caught me off guard when she asked, / *'what colour*

*do you want your cast?' / 'pink. i think. yeah, that'll be cool.' / i don't
care about the boys at school, / oh doctor lady, all i care about is you /
but the boys didn't care about the colour of the cast, / wrote messages
that'd last / for twelve whole weeks about getting better sooner.*

*when i was fourteen i broke my brain / a depressed slide into the dark
side will do that / no doctor lady could fix this break / no gas could I
take / that would take me away to another place / i was in the corner
of a doorless space / no stars / no light / no gravity / i fell / waiting for
the pen marks on the cast around my thoughts / to heal what i had
broken / but the only cast was me: outcast / weakened by a stigma /
wrapped in a taboo / wound so tight it nearly killed me.*

*i learned i can break my body but not my mind / i can break my bones
but not my brain / i was depressed / that does not make me less / i am
sick / not getting better sooner / or perhaps i am / because i'd sooner
be alive than not.*

*every day i battle to wrap casts around breaks that no one can see /
every day i battle /*

every / single / day.

I finish. They all clap. Norma and Andy cheer and
Mum and Susan are both crying. I blush and laugh,
embarrassed, when I get back to them. 'A new one?
Why didn't you warn us?' Mum sobs, smiling and
hugging me tight. I shrug.

To me it doesn't feel that new. I wrote it about a year
ago, but this is the first time I've shown anyone. Something happens when I write stuff down, it stops whirring
around in my head and becomes this tangible thing that
I can look at and prod and get used to. And get over,

I suppose. When I first wrote this poem I was sure I'd never show anyone; even writing the word 'depressed' was hard because it was like admitting something. But the more I read it, and the more time that passes, it just becomes a poem. Something I made rather than a confession or a part of myself. Tonight when I read it, it was just a poem.

A poem that got an honourable mention and a ten-dollar voucher to a coffee shop. Who said the life of an artist wasn't glamorous?

When we get home there's a letter for me. A white envelope with my name quickly scrawled on the front and nothing on the back. Not even a stamp. I rip it open.

Dear Gideon,

Thank you for your letter. It made me laugh, especially the part about me being cool, you idiot. Um. No. Is it bad letter etiquette that in the second sentence of my letter I've called you an idiot? Or are we even now because you called me weird?

Sorry for calling you an idiot. If this was real life and my dad had heard me say that I would've been grounded for sure. He has lots of rules about what is appropriate.

Seeing as you like lists, I've compiled one of all the things my dad thinks are unacceptable.

Ways to piss off Ava's dad: a list
(it's mostly just a list of words he immensely dislikes—see, this is the best example because he hates the word hate so you have to say immensely

dislike). He also immensely dislikes the words idiot (sorry again), stupid and wog. I feel like I'm not as skilled as you at writing lists. He immensely dislikes the word wog because he's Greek, which by the laws of genetics means that I'm Greek too.

The only time I can remember writing letters is to my Yiayia when I was little because they live down south. I should probably still write to her. But she calls once a week and sings me 'You Are My Sunshine'. That's our song. She's pretty funny, mad about the pokies and deep-fried food, and she's really racist. My Pappou is quiet and grumpy and he barely says a word, unless it's about Family Feud which is his favourite show ever. If it ever gets cancelled God help the people in that office. My dad and his brothers were all born here in Australia and they're all still down south, it's just me and Dad up here.

How are you enjoying the wonder that is Magic Kebab? You've lasted longer than any other dishie Ricky has hired so you should probably get a certificate or something for that achievement. Leave it with me.

I don't like snakes either. But I love bananas. How do you feel about mangos or avocados or lychees? They too have protective coverings. There's not very many foods I don't like, except caperberries, I think they're foul, but you don't seem to come across them all that often so, you know, props to my taste buds for that one.

So, Gideon, tell me more about this no phone

or internet or acting normal thing. I'm intrigued.

Thanks again for writing, I thought for sure you were bullshitting when you said that you would so it was a nice surprise to actually get your letter. It's super late and I can't sleep so soz for my rank handwriting. Are letters just an excuse for ranting? I feel like I'm ranting. Can you even read my handwriting? You have nice handwriting. I feel like I have shit handwriting. I don't know what else to say.

Love Ava

P.S. Write back. If you, you know, wanted. I hope you do. ☺ ☺ ☺

P.P.S. I hand delivered this because I didn't know where to buy a stamp. And then I felt like the dumbest person alive and didn't want to ask. And then I realised on the way here that normal people buy stamps at a post office. But I've never been to a post office so I don't know where one is and then I had like an existential life crisis about technology and my involvement in the world because I just looked up your address on my phone and then I realised I could've done that with a post office. Long story short, your house is nice.

Ax

My insides quickly pump out this feeling of giddy happiness, like pumping soap from a bottle—it's quick and squishy and makes me feel better about myself. She is directly mocking me with her P.S. and I like it. She wants me to write back, which means that my letter wasn't a complete disaster. I wrote four drafts before I sent it. I could actually recite it off by heart by the time I put it in the envelope. I feel like Ava did not write four drafts. I feel like this is the one and only copy of this letter. I really like that idea. Like, there's a chance that she's probably forgotten what she wrote but I have it, and now only I know. I was so nervous that mine would go down like a lead balloon and it would make everything more awkward at work, but not only did it go down well, but she wrote back and she even wants me to write again.

This is actually the best-case scenario, which is a place I'm not used to being in. I feel like some kind of intrepid traveller who's just landed in a new place and I need to quickly work out how to navigate this new and tricky terrain and where exactly I should plant my flag as a sign of me being there. In this instance my flag will be my second letter. I feel like I might need to take a different approach this time around and just write it and send it and not think too much about it because I'm all too aware of my propensity for obsession and if I fuck it up, well, that will mean no flag and no Ava.

So, I just need to write it and send it like in class with Ria. We do stuff like this all the time. Ria is all about diving in and seeing what happens. You're not allowed to make justifications about what you write or make. 'You apologise too much, Gids,' she yelled at me once. Her hair was fluorescent orange at the time. 'If you start another sentence in the class with the word "sorry" I will body-slam you,' she joked as her wicked smile cracked her pink cheeks.

'Sorry. Okay,' was my reply and she came running at me, laughing.

'The only time you need to apologise is if you offend someone or you physically hurt them.'

'Or if you fart,' Andy added and everyone cracked up laughing.

Ria thought this was hilarious. 'Yes, great; they're the only times, got it?' Everyone nodded as Ria quickly turned to me, the light catching the glint of her diamond septum piercing. 'Got it?'

'Yes.' You don't argue with Ria.

'You do not need to apologise for being on the planet. You have a right to be here. What you have to say is valid. We want to hear it. None of this bullshit martyr stuff. Own your art. Own your existence. Don't be dickheads. Simple?' Ria mimed dropping a microphone on the floor as we all shouted with glee.

Now, with her words ringing in my ears, I get the timer out of the kitchen and put it on my desk. I give myself thirty minutes. Whatever I write in thirty minutes has to go in the envelope. In the envelope that I will address and stamp so it's ready to put in Mum's handbag in her room so she can stick it in the post tomorrow and I won't be tempted to mess with it. If I can do this it'll be the greatest act of willpower I've ever enacted. I spin the dial on the timer and I start to write. It's kind of difficult at first, but then I start to ramble about all sorts of things and get on a roll. It dings. I sign my name.

From Gideon.

I don't read it back, I just fold the letter up, put it in the envelope, seal the flap and give it to Mum with the explicit instruction to post it tomorrow and under no circumstances is she to listen to future Gideon when he asks for it back.

I don't ask for it back and I barely sleep thinking about it and all of the possible disastrous ways it could go.

•

'How are you?' Robbie asks. Today he has a denim vest on with all of these obscure badges pinned all over it. There are flat, colourful versions of the Golden Girls staring back at me as I say, 'Good,' and he throws a stress ball that's shaped like the world at my head.

'Try again, doofus.'

'School is fine. Home is fine. I am fine. I had one micro-episode last week but I've made some pretty impressive out-of-character choices, so that's good.'

'Tell me about the episode.' He rests his hands on his stomach and as he does the Betty White pin bounces slightly so it looks like she's nodding. I tell him about the panic attack I had after my driving lesson. The instructor had asked me to parallel park on a busy street. I got super nervous because I am awful at parallel parking and then this car came up behind me and stopped and I stuffed up my park twice, and then because I knew I was being inconvenient I freaked out and felt like I was disappointing the instructor, also the woman with the blonde bob in the four-wheel drive. I got all flustered and just pulled out, told him I couldn't do it, drove home and sat in my room for hours feeling like my chest was being crushed by a large boulder.

'I think it's interesting that you're more concerned about the lady in the four-wheel drive than you are about yourself.' Robbie pauses. I wait for some kind of profound wisdom to fall from his bearded mouth but he shakes his head, pissed off. 'Plus she's driving a useless piece of petrol-guzzling machinery for inner-city life and thus she deserves to wait,' he scoffs. 'But that's beside the point. She can see that you're a learner. Why do you think she cared?'

'I just don't want to put anyone out.'

'But you need to learn how to parallel park.'

'Do I though?' I crack and Robbie nods, smiling.

'Would *you* be upset if you were driving and a learner driver was doing a parallel park and you had to wait two minutes before you could continue your drive in your overpriced shitbox?'

He's right. I wouldn't be. I wouldn't care. But this is what my brain does, turns seemingly normal things into moments of high catastrophe. Over the years of therapists, hospital visits, drugs and doctors I've worked out that at any given time I feel one of five possible states.

1. <u>Pre-anxiety.</u> Mild panic. Heart racing. Slightly sweaty. I take deep breaths and feel jittery. The thing with the parallel park and the lady started here. Usually I can use loose mindfulness strategies to talk myself down, but if I can't, well, that leads me into a place of high anxiety.

2. <u>High anxiety.</u> The world is going to end. I can't breathe. I and everyone I care about are most certainly going to die.

3. <u>Hyper-aware.</u> This is like my go-to state, where I'm conscious of everything. I notice details and conversations and remember everything. This is a skill that would probably make me a really outstanding spy or something. But then what tends to happen is I over-process the information I've taken in and assume that everyone is talking about how much they hate me, or how I messed it up, or how my very presence is a hindrance to their capacity to get on with their day.

4. 'Normal' or at least my version of normal, where I can pass as a regular awkward teenager and suppress numbers 1 to 3 to a smaller, more manageable size. They're still present but for these brief moments of reprieve they aren't my most dominant modus operandi. When I'm in class with Ria, when I hang out with Norma and Andy, when I'm writing, when I'm doing my poems live and when I'm at home: these are the times I can pass as normal because I feel normal, albeit fleetingly.

5. <u>Depressed.</u> This feels like flatlining, but not like I'm dying, like my energy is flatlining. I feel nothing. It's like I can't even smile. I imagine myself in this giant see-through cocoon, where I look normal, but everything kind of bounces off the weird external shell, like a banana. Oh man, if I was a fruit I'd totally be a banana. Shit. The thing about being in

the cocoon is that nothing gets in, none of the bad external stuff, but also none of the good. Everything kind of feels muffled. When I'm in it all of the gross stuff on the inside just festers.

Thankfully I haven't been in the full throes of this since I started seeing Robbie and we started to work through some shit and I went on medication. I still have days, or moments or afternoons, where I can feel it creep in, though. Like it's one of those jerks who stands behind you and taps you on the opposite shoulder to them so you turn and look and no one's there. That's what it feels like.

When we finish talking about the freak-out and the parallel park, Robbie asks, 'Now tell me about the good stuff.'

'I've been writing letters,' I tell him and he turns his bearded face to the side like a confused Labrador.

'What kind of letters? Because right now I'm thinking you're sending politically motivated threats to free-to-air TV or something.' He chuckles to himself.

'To a girl.' My heart starts to race.

'Better than trolling Channel Nine. Good. Tell me more.'

I fill Robbie in. I tell him about Magic Kebab and Ava Spirini, how she barely said a word to me for a month until the thing with the MC battle, which I tell him about and he laughs loudly. I tell him about the conversation about letters and the consequent three letters that have since followed.

I don't tell him about Kelly or about Ava telling the whole school to get fucked, or about her wagging. I don't want him to get the wrong idea about her and ask me questions that make me think about things like why she is actually talking to me, and that maybe it's because she's not her normal self right now.

I don't want him to try and make me believe that it's not really a big deal, because it feels like it is, even though I know that it's not because billions of normal people have normal conversations every single day, and for a change I feel like I'm one of them.

I'm enjoying feeling like a normal person. I'm enjoying making a friend. Getting to know someone who knows nothing about me.

'So, she is a heterosexual girl?' Robbie asks, eyebrows raised.

'A real-life one, yes.' I pause. 'I think.' Actually I've got no idea who Ava finds sexually appealing. I haven't wanted to think about it, because it will never be me.

'And you are a real-life heterosexual boy?'

'Yes.'

'So?' Robbie asks, eyebrows raised so high that if they weren't attached they'd most definitely fly off his face.

'No!' I quickly reply.

'No?'

I nod.

'Okay. You seem pretty sure about that.'

'We're not even friends yet.'

'And that's what you want?'

'To be her friend? Yeah,' I say confidently.

'Cool,' Robbie smiles.

Cool? Yeah. It would be. Cool.

AVA

There are three boys staring at me as I sit on the orange plastic chairs wishing I hadn't worn my denim shorts because I'm feeling particularly exposed. They're staring at me through the glass window of a door that leads to a courtyard. The one with a stupid mohawk nods his head in my direction and smiles and the others laugh, patting him on the back. I roll my eyes and give them the finger. They think this is hilarious.

'Hi, Ava.' I spin around and Rahila, the head teacher at TAPs looks at me, then through the glass window out to the boys. She quickly signals them to leave, and they scuffle off.

'So, you've'—she pauses—'met some of our students?'

I nod. She touches the corner of the bright blue head-scarf that sits loosely on her shoulders, then touches my arm. 'Don't be nervous,' she smiles.

I look at her big eyes and her small smile. Her voice is calm and quiet, and I trust her immediately. After our meeting last week I felt better about the whole TAPs idea and if I'm honest I even felt a little excited. I don't need to wear a uniform, there's only forty kids in the whole school, they do shortened days and all of these extracurricular programs that you can be a part of if you want, and you call all of the teachers by their first name. In our meeting Rahila spoke to me, not about me; we had a conversation about what I wanted, what my goals were. I told her I didn't really have any and she said that that should be my first goal, to make some goals. I told her I'd try, and as I said those words, which I meant, I could see Dad's whole body relax a little.

By lunch I feel like I've kind of got an idea of how TAPs works.

'Bullshit, and you know it's bullshit.' Minda, a girl with big pink cheeks and bright green hair is yelling across the room at Allan, a skinny blond boy wearing a backwards cap and a death metal T-shirt.

'Language.' Jason, my new English teacher, smiles, sitting on the edge of a desk.

'No, he's being a dick.' She's grinning though. 'He knew that'd piss me off, he does it every day. He didn't even read the chapter so he needs to keep his mouth shut.' Minda's hand sways wildly in the air as she talks, pointing at Allan, who pulls faces at her.

'I read it. I told you, it was shit,' he mutters.

Minda exhales loudly and Jason jumps to his feet.

'Robust conversation! Yes. This makes me happy.' He slaps the book he's holding. 'Tell me why you think she is immediately prejudiced against him.'

'Because of bullshit stereotypes,' Minda smiles.

'Language,' Jason mutters again and we spend the rest of the class talking about the things that people use to make judgments about us. Jason makes us share one each and I rack my brain to try and think of a good answer. There's only ten people in the group and they say things like their clothes or piercings, hair colour, the music they listen to. Minda talks about her son, who is one, and how everyone thinks she's a skank because she had a kid when she was fifteen. Rae, a girl with short, black, black hair, tells the group that people think because she's fat, she's unhealthy, but then she reminds everyone that she can bench-press some insane number and everyone howls, impressed. Then it's my turn and I don't know what to say.

'Maybe use a personality trait, some way you are, or how you act,' Jason said.

'I'm funny. People think that means I'm happy,' I say.

'Are you?' Minda asks.

'No.' The word spills out of my mouth and my own honesty catches me off guard.

'Join the club, sister.' Minda smiles at me and the others in the class just nod. No one says anything about my answer, no one cracks a joke, and no one even looks surprised. Jason continues with the class as though no grand confession was just made. I instantly feel bad for ever saying stupid or dumb stereotypical shit about

TAPs and the people who go here. I also feel this glimpse of relief peek in to my chest—like sunlight peeking through a window—because no one cares about who I am or what's happened to me because they've all got their own shit to deal with, and this makes me feel incredibly calm. Happy even. Go figure.

•

Two days later I get home from TAPs later than normal because I spent the afternoon with Minda and Rae, who I find out are dating. We go to Minda's house. She lives with her grandma and her son, Maddox, in a small brick duplex. I really like Minda, she's confident and smart. She tells people they're being inappropriate or racist or whatever and she asks good questions, but she's not rude or a dick, it's just like she's got it together. I think she's cool. She adopted me straight after that English lesson on my first day and she's been introducing me to everyone and making sure I know what the deal is.

'Is it weird for you that I have a kid?' she asks, as I hand Maddox a plastic train.

'Not really, you seem like you're good at it,' I tell her. 'I think it'd be weird if I had a kid'—I smile—'but I can barely look after myself right now.'

'You get on with it. You don't really have a choice. Things would be a lot different if I didn't have my nan though.' She smiles as Maddox toddles over to her and gives her the train. 'What's your family like?'

'It's just me and Dad at home; he's great, really awesome actually.'

'You're lucky.' Rae mutters this; she doesn't talk much.

'Yeah, I guess.' It's weird when that happens, when someone says something that makes you realise that what you think is normal really isn't.

I buy Dad a Mars Bar on the way home as a present and write him a note just thanking him for...whatever. Not kicking me out like Rae's parents or dumping me with Yiayia like Minda's mum did when she was little.

There's another mint envelope in the mailbox. I rip it open before I've even put my key in the door and unfold the letter and five stamps fall to the floor. I stand reading it on the porch.

Dear Ava,

First things first and most importantly, I am fine with all fruits, it's just bananas that I think are gross. Phew. I'm glad I was able to get that off my chest and be honest with you. I guess letters are about ranting, yes. Can I tell you something? It's not like you can answer so I'm just going to pretend that you'd say yes. I've given myself thirty minutes to write this letter, I even got the timer out of the kitchen, and I've made a promise to myself to not read it back. I just wanted to write and be honest and not think too much about it. In case you haven't noticed I think a lot, about pretty much everything. I don't know if I should've told you about the timer thing. Obviously I want you to think that I've pondered meticulously over the details in these letters that I've sent you but my friend Robbie is trying to convince me to be bolder, or as he puts it, 'Stop being shy, dickhead.' So, yeah.

As for the phone and internet thing, it's a long and occasionally boring story that I don't particularly want to burden you with. Maybe I'll tell you one day, but the short version is they weren't making me happy, so I thought I'd see if not having them would make me happy. I tend to not really make choices that are based on my own happiness and so I figured I'd start trying to do that a bit more. I don't think I'm one of those people who are naturally happy, you know? I'm definitely not one of those carefree people who go with the flow and wake up every morning in a good mood. I'm not that guy. I tend to live in a state of, well, anxiety. I'm not confident. I know, shock horror, I hardly think you'd have worked that out by now.

I guess what I'm trying to say is that I am fully aware of my foibles, and also that seventeen-year-olds aren't meant to use words like foibles. I don't know what I'm trying to say. Please tell me this makes some sense? Do you like swimming? I think swimming is a perfect example. When we did swimming lessons in primary school I was the kid who would sit on the edge and watch the others playing. I wouldn't jump in. I think it mostly had to do with the story that my sister told me about kids weeing in the pool and that when they did a blue ink spot would appear and follow them around. I was too repulsed by the idea of swimming in wee water to ever enjoy it. Also, I kind of felt duty-bound by this information to sit on the edge and wait for the inky alert so I could tell everyone that it had happened. Maybe I was destined to be a lifeguard. I dunno. Do you want to go to uni? I think I want to do creative writing. I think. Please don't tell Mr Randall I don't know because he's on at us in every life skills lesson about our choices and convincing us that if we fuck up the form we will literally be swallowed by mutant tertiary education zombies and our lives will be ruined forever. I think he's an idiot.

The buzzer just dinged. I hope you're well, Ava. I'll see you at work tomorrow night, but you won't get this by then, so I hope I don't do something dumb and that by some miracle you think I'm more or less normal, only for it to all be dispelled when you finally read this.

From Gideon

P.S. What is this post office in which you speak?

His P.S. makes me laugh out loud. I really like receiving his letters and I quickly try and think back to what he was like at work the other night. We talked a little. Neither of us said anything about writing to each other. We made stupid comments about the drunk people in the shop and he made me laugh with his references to books I'd never read or movies I'd never seen. I like being around him. He just talks to me. He doesn't flirt, he asks me questions or he doesn't say anything at all. There's no expectations or history or weird anticipation about sex or pissing each other off. It's light. It's fun.

I decide to write back straight away. I unlock the front door, take my notebook out of my bag, set the timer on the oven and stand at the kitchen bench and quickly scrawl out my reply. It's long and I'm surprised by how much I tell him.

•

Of all the places in the world where you can have an argument with someone, standing next to the drinks fridge in 7-Eleven on a Saturday night has got to be up there for inspired locations. Other customers keep interrupting you with apologies as they try and get past, or they say nothing, just wrench open the fridge to get their Powerade.

'So what you saying, Aves? You don't want to come?' Lincoln shakes his head, frustrated. We've been circling around this conversation for about five minutes and it's getting more and more heated with every passing second.

'No. I don't. You told me we were just gonna hang out.'

'What do you call this?'

'Fighting in 7-Eleven,' I yell and then glimpse the attendant in his bright green T-shirt staring at us.

'This is not a fight,' Lincoln yells back, his square jaw locking with tension. I groan loudly. I'm so frustrated. Lincoln isn't listening to me. He texted me earlier asking if I wanted to hang out and I told him I didn't want to go out. I was feeling shitty and tired and not up for being around people; he said we'd just hang out, get some food, chill. *Chill* was his exact word. But about two seconds after we pulled into the shop to buy lollies he got a text about some party and he's been trying to convince me to go with him.

'You go, I'll just walk home,' I say, and start to head up the chip aisle.

'No. I'm not going if you don't wanna go,'

I spin back on my heel. 'Why?'

'Cause then you'll be in a shit mood with me for leaving you.' His hands fly from his side and hit his legs with a clap.

'Oh, fuck off, Lincoln.'

'And now you're in a shit mood because I said you'd be in a shit mood. You're a psycho, Ava.' He turns and marches off the other way.

I open my mouth to yell at him and catch a glimpse of my reflection in the glass of the fridge. I barely recognise myself. I've got a giant black hoodie on, the same denim shorts I've worn all week and my Docs, which I haven't even bothered to tie up. My hair is even more wild than normal and the black bags under my eyes are huge. 'Just take me home.'

'Fine.' He marches out of the electronic doors.

'Fine.' I yell back and scurry after him.

We sit in the car and don't talk; I keep my head turned away from him and look out the window. He drives fast, faster than he should, speeding around corners and slamming the brakes so the whole car jolts.

'Don't be a dickhead,' I grit, but he doesn't say anything.

Being with Lincoln is the complete opposite to being around Gideon. There's nothing but history and expectation and he flirts with me one minute and then cracks the shits with me the next. I never know what to expect.

He pulls up out the front of my house and I unclick my seatbelt and look at him. He's gripping the steering wheel so tight his knuckles have turned white.

'Why are you so pissed?' I ask.

He bites the side of his cheek then spits: 'I dunno what you want.'

'What do you mean?'

'I dunno.' He turns his head but doesn't look at me. 'Just get out.'

My throat constricts and I swallow hard and the words fly out. 'Fuck, you're a jerk.' I grab the doorhandle with such force that I'm pretty sure it'll snap off. Lincoln takes hold of my arm.

'No. Shit, Ava. I'm sorry. Don't.' He stops.

'What?' I pull away and he lets my arm go.

'Can we just...'

'What?'

'Just sit,' he says. 'In the car. And just not say anything for like a minute.'

I huff and sit back, cradling my bag on my lap. He makes me so mad when he can't just say what he thinks or what he wants. It's like I literally see the thoughts flying around behind his eyes. It's like he can't connect them to his mouth, so instead he just ends up getting annoyed and saying weird sentences that don't mean anything.

I listen to him breathe. Watch the white of his hands slowly loosen on the steering wheel. Finally, he turns and looks me in the eye and my anger softens too, my shoulders relax. Whatever is happening between us feels so heavy; I have to cross my eyes, and poke out my tongue so we don't have to deal with the weight of it all. He laughs and touches my cheek. Looks me in the eye; slowly leans over and kisses me. Soft at first but then I feel his other hand on my face as we kiss harder and he holds me gently against him. I pull away and we breathe quickly, then I lean over and kiss him again. The handbrake digs into my leg but I don't care. It's frantic and messy and noisy. It's so hot. I feel Lincoln's hand moving up my thigh and his fingertips edge the hem of my shorts moving to the inside of my leg and then suddenly I become all too aware of where we are and what we are doing.

I pull away and place my hand on top of his. 'I'm gonna go.'

'What?'

'Yup. I'm going inside.'

'Do you want me to come with you?' He's undoing his seatbelt.

I pause, picking up my bag, open the car door again and put one foot on the road. I don't look at him.

'No.' I shake my head and get out of the car. I faintly hear a frustrated groan as I march up the porch and into the house.

•

'You're home early,' Dad mutters from the couch.

'Yeah, I feel a bit sick.' I smile at him so he knows I'm okay and go straight to my room.

A bit sick is an understatement: I feel like a fucking idiot. Lincoln is right, I am a psycho. I don't understand how I can go from hating him with such rage that I'd be happy to never see him again to like, one second later, be making out with him in the car directly outside my house. About fifty metres away from my dad who, if he felt so inclined, could have looked out the front window and seen his daughter starring in her very own porno.

I didn't even want to go out. Now Lincoln is going to be super pissed and I'm going to have to deal with that. And what are we even doing? I know he doesn't like me like that. I'm positive about that, at least I think I am. The last time we hooked up I kind of made a pact that I wouldn't let it happen again, that we needed to just hang out like normal friends, but I can't help it when he looks at me with his black-coffee eyes and perfect lips, I just turn into some sex fiend incapable of making rational decisions.

My thoughts feel like they're floating outside of my head and I'm trying desperately to catch one of them but there's too many and they're flying too fast, and I don't know how I feel about anything. I lie down on the bed and stare at the ceiling.

'Are you okay?' Dad asks, standing in the doorway.

'Yeah.' But it's a lie. I am not okay.

GIDEON

'You are an amazing specimen of a man and I am glad that you are here.' Andy greets me at the door wearing a tiara and bright green blazer.

'I didn't realise we were getting dressed up.'

'What? This old thing?' He laughs, his eyes wild. He wraps his arm around my shoulder and ushers me into the kitchen, where he thrusts a white plastic cup into my hands.

'What is it?'

'Wine. Drink. Don't whine.' He grabs my hand and leads me downstairs to the lounge room, where there is a large picnic blanket on the floor and a heap of people from class. Andy in his tipsy state decides to announce my arrival as we reach the bottom stairs.

'GIIIIDDDDDDDEEEOOONNN,' he slurs loudly and Norma cheers. The others, about eight people in total, smile and wave and I perch myself on the edge of the couch and make a promise to myself to try to have a good time.

Everyone is drinking out of their own white plastic cups and they all seem to have quite cheery dispositions so I figure I may as well join in too. I take a big swig. It tastes like vinegar.

The rest of the night moves as expected. I even have fun—we sit on a blanket on the floor and talk about movies and politics and music and Ria. We keep drinking the cheap wine, giggling, repeating ourselves far too many times. I'm still oddly aware of drinking too much but also have this kind of fuzzy filter over everything where it moves a bit slower and everything is a bit more confusing and I am exponentially funnier, or at least I think I am. In fact everyone thinks I am because they laugh and occasionally yell things like 'Yeeeessss!' which I quite enjoy.

At one o'clock in the morning we decide to make pancakes, which just results in a pancake batter fight. Issy scones me right in the forehead with a handful of flour and so I grab her and lift her up around her waist and put her over my shoulder. I feel like Tarzan, helped of course by the fact that Issy is like the tiniest of all tiny teenage girls. She squeals and giggles and pats my butt as I ask the others in the fight, 'Has anyone seen Issy?'

Eventually we run out of flour and Andy has a moment of lucidity and looks around the mess in the kitchen and we all stare at him in silence as he takes it in and then starts laughing. His parents don't get back for a week so we've got time to clean up.

And then we're all out in the backyard attempting to get the flour out of our eyes and hair. Everyone strips down to their underwear and runs under the hose. I do not and quickly head for the bathroom. The giggly buzz I was feeling drops like one of those cartoon two-ton weights and hits my stomach like a thud. I lock the bathroom door and wash my face. I do not need them to ask me why I'm not getting undressed like the rest of them. When I go back out everyone is saturated, shivering, near naked and tired. I smile and find towels for them, trying to be as polite with my eyes as possible and not lose my mind about the sight of girls in wet undergarments. I've been to the beach—I've seen real-life girls in bikinis before, but this feels different. I don't know why because it's the exact same amount of fabric covering the exact same amount of flesh on their bodies but this feels intimate, like I shouldn't be looking even though every cell in my entire body wants to.

Later, when we're back downstairs and everyone is a little less exposed, I sit on the couch observing. Norma sitting on Andy's lap, Tess and Suvi on the floor, resting their heads on the same cushion, which sits delicately perched in Che's lap, Neil sound asleep in the recliner. Issy plops onto the couch next to me and hovers her legs over my lap so she can put them down. I lift my hands and she rests her legs on my thighs. BUT WHAT DO I DO WITH MY HANDS NOW? I'm going to look like an idiot if I don't put them down soon. I try to appear nonchalant about resting my forearms across her shins.

'Gids? Who?' someone says.

'Who what?'

'In this room. Marry, fuck, kill?' Che announces, his eyes squinting because he lost his glasses in the great food fight of 1 a.m. and now can't really see anything, plus he's the only one still drinking the wine.

'I'm not answering,' I bumble.

'We're all answering, you have to,' Suvi gruffly says from the floor. 'I've already gone.'

'Who were yours?' I ask.

'Fuck Issy, marry Tess and kill Neil.'

'You're killing Neil because he's asleep?' I ask.

'He's a liability. What if we were in the jungle and he was on lookout?' Everyone nods. 'I can't have that kind of negativity in my life.' We all laugh and then quickly quieten down so as not to wake the now hypothetically murdered Neil.

'You raise a good point, Suv, so I'll kill Neil.' My butt clenches as I quickly try to come up with a joke to get through the next two. 'I'd marry you, Suvi, because you have this whole jungle scenario worked out and I feel like you could protect me.'

'And who are you going to humpty hump?' Andy murmurs from the couch.

'I dunno.'

'You do, just say it.'

'No, I'm a gentleman and—' They cut me off, yelling at me to answer, until finally I mutter, 'Issy.'

'Why does everyone want to fuck me?' she laughs, and I blush.

About two hours later Issy and I are the last awake, which for anyone else would probably seem like an excellent opportunity to hook up. I mean she didn't run away screaming when I announced that, if pressed, out of the girls in the room I would choose to be intimate with her. She then in turn chose to marry me.

'I think Gideon would be a great husband,' she announced to the group and then my hand disconnected with my brain and just decided to do its own thing and respond by awkwardly patting her leg. The un-sexiest thank-you gesture in the whole history of thank-you gestures.

Neil is still asleep on the recliner, unaware he's been chosen seven times to be killed. Tess, Suvi and Che share one doona on the floor, and Andy and Norma have gone up to Andy's room. Not before making Issy and me stand up so they could pull out the sofa bed.

This is why I now find myself in a bit of a predicament. A predicament that is shaped like a sofa bed with a very pretty girl lying next to a very awkward boy. He has no freaking idea what to do, so for the last hour or so he has done nothing. Zero. Zilch. Nada. In fact he has focused so much of his attention on the exact location of his limbs in relation to the girl lying next to him that he has barely paid attention to any of the things she's tried to talk about. Instead the boy has been uttering caveman-like one-word answers or grunts.

'Are you tired?' she asks.

'Mmm hmm.'

'I'm not. Or I am, but I'm not, you know?'

Do it, Gideon, make a move, seal this deal, you don't know if the opportunity will ever come again. Roll over, touch her, say something. Quick, do it now before the chance is gone and you have to wait another seventeen years. I go to make a move and then immediately back off and try to make it look like I just rolled over. At least I'm now facing her. Issy is lying on her back and I'm so close to her that I can feel the heat of her skin.

'Do you think people realise how ridiculous the saying "have your cake and eat it too" is? Because obviously if there is cake I'm going to eat it.' She laughs nervously.

'I've never thought about it,' I say as my brain and my body line up in perfect synchronicity and we go for it. We make our move.

Our move, as it turns out, is to rest our arm over Issy's mid-section with a kind of heavy thump, leave it there for about, oh, six seconds, say the word 'Night', and then scuttle off to the other side of the bed. Leaving Issy to probably question what on earth just happened and surely be convinced that I do not know how to hug properly and cutting all potential opportunities for any other engagement this evening.

SUCH. AN. IDIOT.

I do not sleep at all. Instead I lie there pondering all of the possible and much better ways that tonight could've gone, and repeatedly and with great energy berate myself for even thinking I could be cool enough to pull that off.

I also mull over the grandest question of them all. Is it always going to be this hard?

•

Robbie and I are laughing, the loud, raspy kind of laughter where you can't breathe and the tears come out. I told him all about my failed moves at Andy's place on the weekend and at first we talked about insecurity, about my propensity to overthink things, about my general belief that I'm a failure as a man.

We processed all of that, and then Robbie said this: 'It's never not nerve-racking. But then there's also an element of it that's meant to be easy, and that's when you know it's right. When you can sit in that sweet spot between freaking out and being at ease.' He smiles. 'This does not sound like that.'

I nod. It wasn't easy. At all. In fact if I'm honest I don't actually think I want to make out with Issy at all. Yes, she's pretty and I find her attractive. Yes, there was an opportunity and yes, I think if I hadn't done the good old split-second arm hug then there's a high probability that she would've kissed me back. But I didn't want to. I feel an enormous amount of relief and my body feels lighter. I smile at Robbie and that's when we start to crack jokes back and forth about my shithouse moves.

'It's like a bad wrestling move,' Robbie grins.

'If I'd done it any harder I probably would've winded her.' I shake my head and laugh, watching Robbie as he struggles to catch his breath.

'Okay, okay, stop. We have to stop,' he eventually mumbles, exhaling loudly. 'You're gonna be okay, mate, like actually, like expert opinion, I believe it.' He smiles at me.

'Thanks.' I nod and I don't really believe him but it's nice to know that Robbie thinks it. I probably care about his opinion more than anyone's, especially more than my own.

'And now, there's something that I've got to tell you, and it's a bit hard for me,' Robbie says. His eyes are scanning my face.

'Okay.' I try to read his body language, get a sense of what he's going to say, but he's his usual calm self. I immediately go to worst-case scenario and in the second-long pause convince myself that he's got cancer and is going to die.

'I'm moving,' he says.

I feel relieved that it's not anything worse, and that his life isn't in danger, but then the pendulum in my brain flips back and I think about myself, and if without him I'll in fact be the one in danger. Robbie is telling me about a fellowship that he's won at some fancy American university where he's going to go and do some research project. He tells me that he's not leaving for a few months. He tells me that we can still Skype and that he's happy to make recommendations about other people for me to see, and that we've got time to process this and what it means for me. Robbie, as always, makes me laugh and feel at ease and does his best to convince me that everything is going to be okay. He does such a good job that I almost believe it's all going to be okay.

•

I feel weird when I get home. Like I should be sad about Robbie's news, but I don't feel sad. I go up to my room and there's a letter from Ava and a postcard from Annie sitting on the corner of my bed. I feel relieved that she's replied. It's been a few days and I was convinced that she wasn't going to.

Gideon,

I am now timing myself too and agree to the thirty-minute, no-reading-back limits that you've placed on yourself. But before I started writing I had to look up what the word foible meant. I looked it up on my phone. You know, like a normal person who has a phone? I don't know what your fascination with being normal is. I don't think any of us are normal. We've all got shit going on, but we're all trying to convince each other that we're normal. I think it's fucked. I think it would be so much better if we were all just more honest and said when things were bad, or that we weren't okay or we were sick or we were happy or whatever. I used to be one of those people you talked about. One of those people who would wake up in a good mood. I think it's just in you, you know? You're either a positive person or you're a negative person. I was a positive person. I'd see the good in everything and believed in bullshit sentiments like everything happening for a reason. But then, some shit went down, and I don't know if I feel that way anymore. I feel like I've kind of learnt that the world can be completely awful and once you learn that I don't know how you unlearn it. I don't know how everything becomes okay again.

I don't know if you know this but I'm not at school anymore. I got expelled for punching Trevor Lane in Maths. I've started at TAPs and I've only been there a few days but I think I like it. I think it's gonna be way better than having to listen to Mrs Bryan lie about her concern for me. I don't know if I want to go to uni. I don't know what I want to do when school is done. You must be so excited being so close to being finished. If your letters are anything to go by then I think you're already an amazing writer. I don't know any other poets.

Past Ava, the girl who was kind of happy all the time, she had a plan to go travelling and see the world and go on adventures and stuff but I don't know if I want to do that anymore. In fact it feels kind of exhausting. All I know is I don't want to be at Magic Kebab forever. Don't get me wrong, I think Ricky is so fucking awesome, but he's crazy. Then again he does love it. I don't think I feel that way about anything yet. I don't love anything the way that Ricky loves meat on a stick. I used to love swimming. In like Year 7 and 8 I was mad into it and would get up early every morning and do squad training. I even had personal best times and shit. I don't even think I own a pair of swimmers now. I don't know how I feel about that. I got told the story about the inky wee spot in the pool, but rather than sit on the edge I tested the theory and so instantly knew that it wasn't true. I don't know what that says about me and you.

I think it's awesome that you want to be happier, Gideon. I really do. I've kind of realised how miserable I am. Maybe I'll tell you all about it one day. You can tell me the phone story and I'll tell you about this year. Deal? One thing that I do know that makes me happy, even for a moment, is your letters. Thank you for the stamps. And for the record, you weren't weird at work. Okay, maybe a little, but I like it. You make me laugh. I'm sorry I'm such a miserable bitch all the time.

See you at work on Friday.

Be happy, Gideon.

Love Ava

P.S. I wrote well and truly over the timer. I'm a rebel like that.

I've never really thought about how shit things must actually be for Ava right now. She does a relatively good job of hiding it. Apart from that time at assembly, and I didn't know that she'd punched Trevor. I'm not exactly in any kind of circle at school where I'd hear that. But I do know who Trevor is and he's a wanker so I feel pretty safe in assuming he deserved it. I've never been in a fight. I wouldn't know what to do. Annie would get into fights for me if I ever needed her to. I remember her postcard, it's a photo of the queen.

You'd love London like I love you, which is lots and lots.

I hope you're being brave, little brother.

Love Annie

Brave? I think, smiling about the possible reply I'll create later for her.

Oh, Annie, I'm practically a superhero for all of the bravery I've been swinging around these parts of late.

I slept with a girl.

Or at least she slept while I lay wide awake pondering the bold failure of my arm-toss-count-to-six failed sex move which, shockingly, didn't work. But never mind because I have been writing letters to another real-life girl where I divulge information about myself and don't vomit. In fact, I think I'd go as far as to say that she is my friend. I've made a new friend, Annie, is that brave enough for ya? Oh, and Robbie is leaving and I didn't have a mental breakdown about the news. So, brave? Yes.

Your brother,

Gideon

AVA

I sit on the edge of Lincoln's bed. I promised myself I wouldn't have sex with him. That we'd just hang out and sort out the mess from the other night, but he didn't bring it up, and so I didn't bring it up and then he kissed me and I didn't stop him. I didn't want to stop him. I pull my singlet over my head and am met with a barrage of yuck feelings. It's like someone has turned on a tap and they fill me up and make me dizzy: guilt, regret, sadness all sloshing about making me numb and sick, like the moment just before you spew. I can feel the blood leave my body, I get cold and clammy and my mouth just starts pumping out way too much saliva as my stomach starts churning. That's pretty much what I feel like whenever Lincoln and I hook up. After, I mean. When it's actually happening it's great.

I turn and look at him, lying shirtless on the bed

with the sheet sitting on his hips. He's looking at something on his phone.

'Lincoln?' I ask.

'What?' He doesn't look at me.

'Do you think—'

'What?'

'Do you think she'd be mad at us?' I rush out. We very rarely talk about her. But I want to. I so desperately want to know what he thinks, to see if his insides are churning too.

'I don't care what she thinks.' He still doesn't look at me, just stares at the phone above his face.

'You do.' I turn around and lie on my stomach on the bed near him and immediately he gets up and picks a pair of shorts up off the floor.

'I don't'—he pauses and finally looks at me for the first time—'because she clearly didn't give a flying fuck if any of us would be mad at her.' He picks up a shirt off the carpet. It's inside out and he tries to fold it out the right way but his hands move too quickly and he just ends up pegging it across the room. 'I hope she's mad at me. I hope she's furious,' he says, staring at the shirt on the floor.

I sit up and cross my legs. 'I hated it when she was mad at me.'

'She was never mad at you.' Lincoln softens a little and breathes heavy.

I watch his chest move quickly up and down. 'Yeah, she was. When I wouldn't follow along with one of her crazy plans or I'd be too much of a pussy to say things.'

I pause. 'Or when I'd ask her to tell me how she really felt she'd just get mad at me.'

'You should've made her.' His eyes look hollow and he bites the corner of his lip.

'Should've made her tell me?' I scoff. 'I couldn't make her do anything.' I pull at a loose thread on the blanket. 'None of us could.'

Lincoln turns his back and raises his hands above his head. He grips one hand with the other and rests them on his forehead and sighs loudly. 'You could've.'

'No,' I tell him, but he rushes over the top of me.

'She trusted you. She loved you.' He closes his eyes, shakes his head. Turns away. Under his breath he says, 'But you let her die.'

'What?'

It's like he's punched me in the guts and I propel my body forward, standing up. 'You think this is my fault?'

'No. I didn't mean that.' He shakes his head, agitated.

'You did.' I grab his shoulder and turn him around to face me. 'You did mean that.'

'No. I'm sorry,' he mutters and tries to wrap his arms around me but I push at his chest.

'You don't care about me.'

'You don't know what I'm feeling, Ava.'

'That's it though, Lincoln. I do.'

'She was *my* sister—' he screams, and he takes a step towards me with his finger in my face.

I cut him off. Push his hand out of the way. 'SHE WAS MINE! I know EXACTLY how you feel. Exactly,'

I yell louder than I've ever yelled before. How dare he. I'm furious. My hands start to shake. 'Fuck you, Lincoln.' I pick my shorts up off the floor and quickly step into them.

'You already did,' he whispers.

I spin around and with all my strength push my hands into his chest. I'm so angry. He pushes me back and I land on the bed and I kind of bounce so the side of my face hits the bedside table. The pain is immediate. I hold my cheek. I'm bleeding. My heart is racing and all I can smell is cigarettes and spit as I close my eyes, shaking my head.

He crouches down in front of me straight away and touches my leg. 'Ava I'm sorry—'

I pull away. 'Don't *touch* me,' I hiss. I fold my knees under my body and stare at him. Neither of us moves.

'I just—Ava?' He softly touches my arm and I reef it away.

'No,' I sob and it all comes pouring out in a mess of tears and snot, 'you don't care. You don't care about me. Why? Why are you doing this?' I look at him as my heart pours out onto the bed and all over Lincoln, who just sits there. Scared. 'You never have and you are a bad person and I am a bad person for doing this and I should've told you. I should've told you—I should've said no but you should've known not to do it. But I let you. And this is all my fault because I wanted to feel like shit. I did it cause it hurts,' and I cry. Cry like the moment I found out that Kelly died, cry because it's the only thing I can do. Cry because every single part of me hurts. 'It hurts all the time, and I just miss her. I miss her so much.' I hit my chest with my hand and quickly cover my face.

Lincoln sits up on his knees and grabs me hard and tight around the waist and I push him away with every bit of strength I can muster. I don't want him to touch me. I try and wriggle away but I can't, he's too strong. He clings to me so I kind of fall into it, into him, sobbing, howling, crying into his shoulder. He holds me and when I finally catch my breath a bit I sit back and look at him and he stares at me, like right at me. He says, 'I miss her too. She would hate me right now. Hate this. Us.'

I nod, looking at his face. This is the look, the sad look, the small open gateway where he lets me in for just a moment. He's being honest. And he's right. She would hate it, maybe not us, but this, that we were fighting. That I was crying, him being vulnerable and me being a bitch and us sleeping together when we didn't really want to, when we didn't really like each other. Not like that.

'And everything is so fucked. And you are...so—'
He pauses.

I'm so what? He doesn't finish the sentence.

'And she's gone. Yeah? She's really, actually gone.'

I'm breathing heavy and he just looks so.

Sad. So sad. He looks how I feel. So I tell him what I really think.

'Sometimes I think she's still around.'

He pauses. 'She's not. She's dead.'

And like that the look is gone and the gap is closed and he's back to being wound so tight, like the cork in a bottle you just shook up. He breathes in deep. 'I don't think I'll ever get over this.' And he buries his head into my lap and I don't need to look at his face because I can feel it in his body, in his shaking chest, in his yelps, that Lincoln is crying too. I wrap my arms around his back, grabbing on to him and he holds me too. His knees kind of falter and it's just me holding him as he howls.

I don't notice the sound of the front door opening. I don't notice Tina yelling out to Lincoln. I don't notice her opening the door to his room. I don't notice till she's right in front of me, staring at me, looking at me with big brown eyes just like Kelly's and she doesn't say anything just lifts my hand off Lincoln's shoulders and takes his weight and she falls onto the floor with him.

Her scrambling to sit as Lincoln wraps his arms around her waist and sobs into her lap.

And she cries and strokes his head and tells him it's all going to be okay and I just sit on the edge of the bed and watch them. Lincoln's dad appears and kneels next to them with one hand on Lincoln, his tears welling and distorting his strong hard face. Tina looks me right in the eye and I just stare back at her and I can see it in her eyes that she's broken too, and she sees it in me and she knows. I know she knows exactly how I feel.

I can't remember them walking me into the lounge room, or lying down on the couch and falling asleep.

All I remember is waking, startled, with Dad stroking my hair. He asked me if I wanted him to carry me to the car. I remember because it made me smile and that it felt weird to smile.

'I haven't had to do that since you were about six, but I will if you want me to,' he smiled. I just shook my head.

It's 3:31 a.m. when I wake up and look at the clock in my room. Dad is sound asleep next to me, still wearing his shoes. I feel hungover and empty. I have a pain in my head that smashes into the back of my eyes every time I move. I'm thirsty but I don't get up, I just roll over and listen to Dad snore.

It's the best sound in the world listening to him breathe. I do feel like I'm six years old again. Like when I'd just had a nightmare and nothing felt like it'd be okay, but Dad would lie with me and crack jokes about rescuing me from whatever bad thing had happened. He'd tell me over and over again that he'd be able to defend me because monsters, or robbers, or sea witches weren't as powerful as a dad, and I believed him. I'd lie there and listen to him breathe and even though I felt completely unsettled I knew it would be okay, because I knew I was safe.

Only now I don't feel safe, not really, because bad shit can happen and there's nothing anyone can do about it. Not even my dad.

•

There are flowers on the welcome mat when I get home from TAPs and I smile because I know they must be from Lincoln and everything is going to be all right. He'll apologise for what happened, then I'll apologise and then everything can go back to the way it was. I haven't seen or heard from him in four whole days, which is the longest we've gone without talking or seeing each other since Kelly died.

I've been walking around in a bit of a daze since our fight, since I hit my face, trying to process what we said and how angry I was, and how good it felt to get a lot of that shit off my chest.

I told Minda I tripped and hit my head on the bedside table—I muttered the words, 'I'm super clumsy.' I did not tell her it's because I was having a fight with my dead best friend's brother right after we'd had sex and he pushed me so hard that I accidentally smashed my face on the bedside table. I don't tell anyone that that's what happened. Not even Dad. I can't quite believe it myself.

I pick up the flowers, relieved, and then I see it, amid the leaves, a mint-green envelope. I instantly feel angry. Angry that they're not from Lincoln and that everything is still up in the air and there won't be any kind of resolution. I'm angry at Gideon for being so nice. I think maybe I've given him the wrong idea. I'm angry because flowers complicate things and he and I aren't meant to be complicated, we're just meant to be friends. I carry them inside and pull out the envelope. I'm confused and grumpy and feel like shit for feeling all of these things because no one has ever bought me flowers before and they're really nice. But, shit, Gideon!

Ava,

I hope these make you smile. I know they certainly can't make you happy, but I figure a smile is a good start. No real letter today—it took me over an hour to work out what flowers I should buy. Flowers are hard.

So here's the dot-pointed version of my so-called life and this so-called letter.

- I've had a few strange days lately. My friend Robbie is leaving town and it's kind of spun me out a bit because I'll miss him.

- There was a party. Something weird happened. That's all there is to say about that.

- Something happened at work on Sunday when you were away. Ricky said you were sick. I hope you feel better. So, Ricky showed me the tattoo on his butt. I don't know how to feel about this. 1. Because I've now seen how hairy his arse is and 2. Because of what it's a tattoo of. I don't know if I should tell you because I don't want to mentally scar you too, but solidarity, Ava, solidarity and I've got to tell someone. It's a weird green-looking boxing kangaroo who is shaving a giant shish kebab which actually just looks like a big shit and around the top it says, 'Make Magic'.

If the flowers didn't work, I hope the mental image of Ricky's butt did.

See you on Friday.

Your friend,

Gideon

And despite still being pissed off I crack up laughing. Ricky has threatened to show me the monstrosity that is the artwork on his arse but I have point blank refused to engage and have successfully avoided even knowing what it was for three whole years. I laugh at the mental image of Gideon's face looking at it and Ricky no doubt laughing maniacally. I think I maybe have the wrong idea about Gideon having the wrong idea. Is it actually possible that he just wants to be friends? Everything in me wants to believe this is true.

•

By work on Friday I've decided that I need to confront Gideon about the flowers and find out once and for all if he has the wrong idea about us. I can't deal with anything else complicated in my life right now. I figure it's better to know now so I can shut that shit down before it goes any further. I wait for a quiet period in the shop and head out the back to the sink where he's washing up trays.

'Why did you send me those flowers?' I ask—talk about getting straight to the point, Ava, the only other thing we've said to each other tonight is 'hello' and 'hey' and then you bombard him with this.

'What?'

'The flowers? Why did you send me flowers?'

'Because I thought they'd be nice. Why? Should I not?' He stumbles, turning to look at me, holding his hands which are covered in big plastic red gloves in the air.

'No. You shouldn't.'

'Oh, okay.' He looks stung.

'Yeah. Just don't. I don't like flowers.' Which is a lie, I do like flowers but I just want to be clear. Set a boundary, as they say. But looking at his face right now I just feel like shit because I know I'm making him feel bad and that's not actually what I wanted to do at all.

'Oh. Sorry,' he mutters, his eyes look to the ground and he bites his lip.

'It's fine.'

'No it's not. I'm sorry. I just thought you sounded sad. You know. In your last letter and then you were away.' He looks up and the sincerity in his eyes smacks me in the chest and I feel like the biggest bitch in the whole universe.

'Oh, fuck, no, Gideon, thank you. Sorry. Shit.'

'What's wrong?'

'Nothing. Nothing is wrong. Thank you for the flowers. I just thought—' I pause.

'What?'

I don't say anything. I thought they were from Lincoln is what I want to say. I thought Lincoln felt bad about what happened and he sent me flowers to apologise. But he didn't. Because he doesn't feel bad.

I also want to say that I thought he may have thought there was something more between us. That we weren't just two people getting to know each other, as friends. That I thought that the flowers weren't actually just one friend sending another friend an incredibly thoughtful gift because they thought that friend was sad. Because it turns out I'm actually just a psycho bitch who someone so nice shouldn't be friends with anyway.

I realise I've been standing here for a long time not actually saying anything and I both look and feel like an idiot.

Gideon breaks the silence. 'What should I have sent instead of flowers?'

'What?'

'To cheer you up.' He takes the gloves off and wipes his hands on his apron. 'What's your favourite animal?'

'Penguins,' I reply.

'I should've sent you a penguin. I'm an idiot.' He smiles and I smile and feel awful for ever thinking anything bad about Gideon.

'You don't need to send me anything. Just, I don't know. Hang out.'

'Hang out?' he asks, his voice raised a little.

'Yes. Do you want to hang out?'

'I can hang out,' he says, leaning on the sink, but he slips on some detergent and I laugh while he blushes.

'Like friends do. Like friends hang out.' I smile, and he nods and then the bell at the front of the shop goes off and a group of young guys walks in.

As I head towards the front Gideon yells out to me,

'Fine. Gosh. I'll hang out with you, just stop talking about it, Ava. God!'

I turn and give him the finger and he pulls a stupid face at me. Like friends do.

Good.

GIDEON

There's people playing guitars and singing, a human pyramid being constructed, two girls making out, a card game and two guys running around in giraffe onesies. I was wrong. This is not the perfect place to hang out with Ava for the first time.

Norma comes running over, squealing, 'Heeeeeeyyyy!' and jumps onto me. She wraps her legs around my waist and I just stand there and let it happen as she hugs me tight. She jumps down and puts her arm around Ava. 'Ava, welcome to the fourth annual Day in the Park.'

Andy approaches, smiling. 'Have you told her about the initiation?'

'Nope. I thought I'd leave that up to you,' I say.

'Initiation?' Ava asks, looking at me, and I can't tell if the expression on her face is interest or fear.

'Quickly! Get the paddles,' Andy pronounces with a fake British accent.

'Not the paddles, sir, she's too pretty for the paddles.' Norma fans her face with her hands.

I can't help but laugh and Ava looks at me and smiles. I think the look on her face now is one of mild amusement, maybe curiosity, and definitely a little bit of 'what the fuck' thrown in for good measure. Which I expected.

When we agreed to hang out at work the other night I spent three whole days and two whole nights agonising over where said hanging should take place. I asked Andy and Norma in class on Wednesday night.

'Bring her to Day in the Park,' Andy suggested.

'You just want to meet her,' I mumbled.

'Duh!' Norma smiled, nodding. 'But also Day in the Park is good for hanging, it's casual, there's amusing things to talk about and Andy and I can rescue you if you go into one of your awkward spirals of self-loathing.'

I wanted to leap to my feet and hug her. Norma was right about everything and I was so excited about finally having a plan that when I saw Ava at Magic Kebab on Thursday night I was a little too excited about said plan and my brain forgot about the whole sentences that usually begin a conversation.

'Day in the Park!'

Ava spun around and looked at me through the hole in the wall that connects the kitchen to the front of the shop. 'Hello Ava, how are you? Oh, I'm okay, Gideon, thanks for asking.' She stared smugly.

'Sorry. Hello Ava.'

'Hi,' she smiled. 'So, you want to go to the park?'

'Yeah; we could hang out at Day in the Park?'

'You want to spend the day at the park?' Ava asked confused.

'Yes.'

'Okay. We can go to the park if you want to go to the park.'

My heart started racing, I was not being clear at all. 'No, it's a thing that my friends do, it's called Day in the Park, it happens in the park, there's music and food and stuff.'

'Ohhhh.' I see clarity paint Ava's face. She nods. 'I get it. Cool.' She turns around, picks up her phone and continues looking at whatever she was looking at before I crazily interrupted her with my bizarre ramble.

At the end of our shift she told me she'd meet me at my house at midday. We didn't really have a conversation. She asked questions, I answered them and then she left. She's like the freaking caped crusader, only she doesn't wear a cape. Or save people, or...okay, so she's nothing like the caped crusader. I just find her mysterious and I think she's cool, this is the only correlation between her and Batman.

'What do I have to do?' Ava asks, curious.

'You have to come and play Uno with me.' Andy grabs her hand and starts swinging it.

'That's it? I thought you were going to make me do a beer bong or something?'

Norma laughs. 'That's later.'

'Yes, the usual order of proceedings goes Uno, beer bong, paddles,' Andy adds. I watch Ava giggle and be pulled along next to Andy as they skip off to another part of the park.

We play four rounds of Uno with Suvi and Neil as everyone goes about quickly indoctrinating Ava into Prison Rules Uno. There is lots of yelling, pseudo-insults and swearing. Ava stays quiet for most of it but she laughs every now and again. I watch her face as more people join the circle and the conversations jump from topic to topic. We jump from discussing anime to music to gender inequality to an argument about pizza toppings to pronouns of choice and then back to some book that they're all reading. A book which I said I would read but haven't yet, mainly because it's some genre piece about warlocks and sentient princesses, and I figure I've got enough drama in my life already.

Ava listens, she answers questions when she's asked and occasionally makes comments. At first I feel like bringing her here is a terrible, terrible error in judgment but eventually I relax and start to have fun myself.

Later, when everyone runs off to play frisbee, it's just Ava and me sitting on a rug. The group of girls that Issy sits in a circle with keep looking over at us and whispering. I don't think Ava will notice or say anything but if she does I've pre-prepared a couple of responses which

I think will effectively divert the conversation to other, far more interesting places.

'You've got fans,' Ava remarks, looking over at the girls.

Shit.

'No.' I drop my eyes, embarrassed, then try to smile. 'They're called groupies.' This was not one of my pre-prepared answers but I feel like it was excellently executed. I'm even impressed with myself.

Ava laughs loudly. 'Oh, sorry, your groupies love you.'

'Nah. They're just girls from drama. The one with the long brown hair, she does slam too, so yeah.'

'Have you ever had a thing with any of them?' she asks and it lands heavy in the air like a moment of great importance, because if I lie that will set a tone for mine and Ava's friendship from this point on, but I also don't know if I want to tell the truth because that's admitting to a whole other level of personal weirdness. Plus, how do I even answer that question because nothing technically did happen. I look at her and make a choice.

'Issy,' I say quickly, which I think kind of catches her off guard because her head jolts back slightly in surprise.

'Short hair?' she asks, looking over at the three girls.

'Yeah.'

'She's beautiful,' she says, and she means it.

We both look over at the girls; Issy has a frangipani tucked behind one ear.

'We had a weird thing,' I mumble.

And before I have a chance to think about what to say next, Ava asks, 'Did you kiss?'

I shake my head.

'Why not?' She pokes me; I think she's teasing me.

'It was weird. We built it up too much. Too much pressure. I think.' I can feel my eyebrows furrow as I think and watch Ava's eyes kind of glisten as she processes. It's like she travels into the world and then quickly regresses back into her head. I wonder what happens in her brain.

I decide to change the topic. 'How did you do that?' There is a bruise and a little cut on her cheek that I touch gently and can't believe that I did.

Ava's whole body shifts. 'Oh,' she says, covering the bruise with her hand, 'I thought I'd managed to hide it.'

'I noticed it at work,' I say. 'Was it something dumb? I do dumb shit all the time. See this scar on my lip? I got that the one and only time I've used a skateboard. I was seven.'

'Yeah, I rolled into my bedside table, it was dumb.'

All of a sudden a hula hoop appears around Ava's waist and Norma is giggling.

'Do you know how?' she asks.

'Yeah,' Ava says, jumping up and spinning the hoop around her waist and moving her hips to keep it balanced. She knows what she's doing and keeps the hoop up without any effort. 'Is there another hoop?'

'The lady wants another hoop!' Andy yells to the group, and Norma hands it to her. She stops, lines them both up and gets them going. She moves the hoops up to her chest and back to her hips and then she lets them drop, laughing. The group cheers and Ava bows, kind of blushing. 'Your turn.' She points at me.

'I can't. I am completely uncoordinated.' I prove it by shaking my hips violently back and forth as the hoop just drops to the ground.

Ava laughs and sits back on the rug. She tells me a story about her Christmas holidays in Year 7 where she and Kelly learned how to hula hoop because they saw this thing on TV about a girl in the circus.

'She had this incredible costume and could do like ten hoops at once. She looked like an elf.' She's talking quickly, excited, and even if I wanted to I couldn't get a word in. 'We thought she was so gorgeous. She had long curly blonde hair and big boobs and this flat stomach where you could see all of her muscles moving when she hooped. Kelly was just like, I wanna look like her, and I was like me too, and I'd just got fifty bucks from my mum randomly for my birthday and we washed cars to earn an extra twenty and we went and bought two hoops. It took forever to learn. We'd watch videos online and practise for hours.' This is the most I've ever heard her talk; she's so animated her hair bounces around and her hands move wildly.

'Then what?' I ask.

'Then we found something else that took our interest, and I haven't really done it since. I forgot how fun it is.' She stops and lies back on her arms, looking up at the clouds. 'Did you ever do that thing where you'd say what clouds looked like?'

'No. I have no idea what you're talking about,' I say, and she whacks me in the chest. I lie down next to her and look to the sky.

'I think that looks like a koala.' She points up.

'Yes, and that's a dragon.'

'Why is there always a dragon?' she asks, turning her head to look at me.

'One of life's great mysteries.' I turn my head to the side and look at her, we hold eye contact for a second before we break and look back to the clouds. I feel my usual base level of nerves but surprisingly I also feel calm. Like Ava and I are actually friends, like the day is a success, like maybe Annie is right: sometimes all it takes *is* a little bit of bravery.

When we're winding up and everyone is standing in a clump saying goodbye, Norma squeezes Ava. 'Will we see you Friday night?' she asks.

'What's Friday night?'

'Gideon's next comp,' Andy says. 'Has he not told you?'

I blush instantly.

'You have to come, Ava, he's amazing,' Norma adds as Andy is saying, 'Not really, he's actually shithouse, but it's important for us to support his dreams.' He grabs me in a headlock and ruffles my hair.

'I'm rostered on at work,' she says, and I pretend to look disappointed but am actually relieved. Then she says, 'But I'll get it off. I'd like to come.' There's a pause. 'If that's cool?'

'Are you kidding? You're the coolest thing to ever happen to us,' Norma laughs.

Ava's embarrassed and she looks at me while the others keep chatting and insulting each other. She mouths the words *Is that okay?* and I nod big and mouth back *Of course*.

Then I metaphorically shit my pants because today has already used up all the bravery I could muster. Having Ava watch me do one of my poems? That will require a Batman level of bravery.

As Norma links arms with Ava and they walk off ahead, I realise I've got five days to get used to the idea. Crap.

•

By Wednesday I've circled through all of the possible emotions about Ava coming to the competition, all of the possible scenarios of how Friday night could go down and all of the possible poems I could do, and I've landed right back where I was on Saturday, in a state of dread and panic because I have no idea what to expect or what poem to deliver.

'That's easy, doofus, do my favourite,' Annie smiles, all pixelated on the iPad screen.

I've made out that the majority of my anxiety about Friday night relates to not knowing what poem to do. I did not tell Annie that I was freaking out because of Ava being there.

'It's a bit full on.' I lean on the desk and grimace.

Annie looks at me like she's just smelled something

bad. 'Piss off! It's fine. You've never done it for a comp before and it's good.' She pauses. 'Go hard or go home, little brother.' She pulls a stupid face which I respond to by putting both my fingers up my nostrils.

'Are you gonna do it?'

I huff loudly, 'Fine!'

'That was easy. What other shit do you need me to solve for you today?'

'Global warming, political apathy, bad pop music, the guy in my Ancient History class who thought Dubai was in India.'

Annie looks mortified. 'No?'

I nod and she laughs. 'You're on our own with that one. The others I'll sort by lunch. I'll fax you because that's the only way to contact you.'

'Gideon,' Mum shouts from the hallway, 'is she still online?'

'Mum wants you,' I tell her and she smiles.

'I love you,' she says, pulling another weird face. 'Oh, just warn Mum and Suse you're doing the poem.'

At that moment Mum appears in the doorway, 'Gimme, gimme, gimme,' she says, dancing as she picks up the iPad to take Annie out of my room.

A second later Mum pops her hand around the door and throws an envelope at me.

Gideon,

I had a really great time on Saturday. Thank you for inviting me. Your friends are so cool. I don't know if it's okay to have favourites but I really like

Norma and Andy. They were lovely and so funny. And Prison Rules Uno? Oh man. Brutal. I feel like you were all being lenient on me too. Your friends are cutthroat. Ha.

I spoke to Ricky too about Friday and he gave me the night off, but I had to promise that you and I would clean the cold room, which I figure was a worthy compromise until I actually remembered how disgusting the cold room is and then I feared I may have put us in a really shitty position. So, Friday night better be awesome. No pressure. I'm kidding. I'm really looking forward to it. I thought it was amazing that you were smart enough to write poems, let alone get up and read them to people. I don't think I'm that brave.

I stop reading. Brave? Maybe Annie's been sending Ava postcards too.

I get too nervous speaking in crowds of people. Get all tongue-tied and clammy, it makes me feel shit so I just don't do it. Well, unless I'm telling a thousand people to get fucked, but that comes from a different place. Please tell me you have no idea what I'm talking about. Please tell me you weren't at school that day? Oh man. It wasn't my best moment. But I just got so angry with how they had dealt with everything. Like not at all, and Mrs Bryan is a bitch and yeah. What I'm trying to say is I think you're awesome, Gideon. I think it's awesome that you write and that you do slam poetry and I'm glad that Norma and Andy invited me.

I'm having an okay week. TAPs is fine. Good, even. Lots of discussions. I've made a new friend, Minda, she has green hair, a one-year-old kid and she is loud and bossy and smart. She cracks me up. You know what I think the best thing about TAPs is, though? No one knows me. They only know what I tell them. I think even if they did know they wouldn't give a shit. There's some kids in my class who are dealing with the biggest things. There's people who've been kicked out of home, or who are in trouble with the cops, there's one girl who's so shy that she just couldn't cope with being at regular school and another guy, who's in my English class, who's been sober for six months and we had a cake for him the other day to celebrate. He was so stoked. It's just making me realise that everyone has got stuff going on, you know? I don't know what I'm trying to say.

See you Friday, Gideon. I hope your week is awesome too.

Love Ava

I fold the page back up and put it in its envelope. Yes. You are right, Ava, everyone does have their own shit, and you, my friend, are about to learn a little more about mine, whether you like it or not.

•

I hoist myself out of the floral lounge chair and start the walk to the stage. Stepping delicately along the people-lined path as they clap and cheer. Andy and Norma are sitting right at the front and one pats me on the leg and the other pinches my bum. I'm not sure which. They're smiling big and giving me a thumbs-up.

'Hello,' I say into the mic. I look at Ava. She is sitting forward, resting her elbows on her knees with her chin in her hands. Her pinkie fingers sit in between her teeth and she is smiling in a way I've never seen her smile before. Her eyebrows are raised, and her eyes wide.

She's nervous. My capacity to work out how she's feeling hasn't suddenly improved over the course of the evening. I know she's nervous because she told me in the car on the way here, and again at the door when we paid our entry and again when we got a drink and then when we sat down she told me another five or six times.

'Why are you nervous?' I asked.

'I don't know. I just feel, like, jittery.' And she was. Her hands kept clenching and releasing and flying to her hips then her face, then together under her chin. I laughed at her and she pushed me hard in the chest.

'Are you nervous? Do you get nervous?' she asks.

'Yeah. Kind of.' If only she knew the week I'd had in terms of dealing with ALL of the feelings that were swirling around my person about tonight, which I still feel right now and will feel until right up until the moment I open my mouth to perform. When it's happening I don't really feel anything, not until it's over. Then I feel electric, like when your stomach squishes with happiness, only not momentary. It lasts at least the whole night.

'I just—I don't know what to expect.' She pauses and looks at me right in the eye. 'What if you're shit?'

I laugh. 'It's highly probable.'

'No, I mean, what if you are? Then I'm going to have to pretend that it was awesome and you know I'm crap at that.'

'At pretending I'm awesome?'

'Yeah. And lying. I'm a shit liar.'

'Yeah. Just. Don't.' I nod; she cocks her head to one side and looks at me, her hair falling around her face, so I finish. 'Lie. Don't lie.'

'Okay.'

I hadn't really thought about it like that, until she'd said it. What if she does think it's shit? *That I'm shit.*

'I'm Gideon,' I say and I can hear them all wooh and holler. I breathe in through my nose. 'This is called "Head of State".'

I catch Ava's eye, she raises her eyebrows at me; takes her fingers out of her mouth and intertwines them and keeps them rested under her chin. I take a deep breath, clear my throat and close my eyes. Here we go.

surprise attacks / her surprise or mine? / she says it was an accident but the only accident is that it didn't happen sooner / a knitted straitjacket hiding the external / the dark refusing to let in the light / weighed down by a woollen weight so heavy in a summer so bright it burned my mother to her core / she knew, she knew / knew that the polyester telegram emblazoned on my skin was hiding a torment that would cut her soul in half / shocking her till she cried / tears streaming into my flesh / burning my skin / not because of my scars, but the ones i'd just given her.

i came in pain and then again i hurt her / couldn't tell her, 'Mum, i need you' / but i didn't have the words—just tears / now these cries stain the perfect body she made and i can't say anything cause i've been saying it with the tip of a compass, with broken glass / i've been saying it to myself / my mind screaming out for her to pick me up like she would have, pick me up like only she could have / pick me up / pick me up / pick me / pick me and tell me that the dark in my mind, my chest, my heart and skin caused by my hands can be healed with hers.

surprise attacks / she opens the door and she sees me / she / sees / me / like she always has with love in her eyes that hits me so hard straight to my chest that i am winded / by her need to feed, to fix, to find a way to take it all away / wear it on her own shoulders in a click if she could / that's why this woman is / she is.

Queen.

my very own monarch butterfly / flying so high into my head of state / the state that i am in / that she will now rule / cause i'm sick of ruling bleeding lines into my skin.

AVA

Gideon's bedroom is like something out of an Ikea catalogue, all neat and sleek. It doesn't look like anyone actually lives in it, let alone a teenage boy. It even smells nice. There's a double bed that's been made, a desk with squared piles of books and papers. Above the desk is a pin-board with a couple of photos stuck to it; I recognise a few people from Day in the Park.

There's a cupboard with one black and white poster on it; there's a picture of a man with a huge afro and his name, *Gil Scott-Heron*, written underneath in big white letters. I've never heard of him. There's a small table that has a record player on it surrounded by square plastic crates of records. Everything has a place. Even me.

I haven't moved from the same spot on the bed for hours as we've talked and listened to music. I couldn't bear to go home after watching Gideon perform. I had to know more.

He rolls up his sleeves and holds out his arms. Once my eyes adjust to what I'm looking at I can't help it and I take a quick, sharp breath in and lift my hand to my mouth. His arms are covered in thin scars. Ordered and symmetrical, they run up in line with his veins; they're all different lengths.

'How old were you?' I can't help it, I grab his right arm and he kind of flinches but he lets me touch them all the same. There's very little space that the scars don't cover. There are no new cuts, just all these raised white lines like soldiers standing to attention.

'Um, five years ago it started.' Gideon pulls down his sleeve.

I don't move, I'm so confused. I know he said he'd had some stuff happen but I didn't realise how bad it was for him. 'How?' I ask.

'I'd do things like "accidentally" break a glass in the kitchen, and then I'd keep shards in my pocket when I cleaned it up.'

'Did your parents know?'

'Not for ages.'

''Cause one of your mums? The poem. Yeah?'

'Yeah.' He smiles. 'We went on a holiday. To the Barrier Reef. Lots of snorkelling and that. In the middle of summer. I refused. Just sat. Long sleeves. And yeah, Mum, Susan, walked in on me in the bathroom.'

'Doing it? Cutting?'

'No. But I'd just got out of the shower. She saw

my arms. I think she suspected when I wouldn't take my jumper off the whole trip.'

'You think she did it on purpose?'

'She said it was an accident—'

I cut him off. *'But the only accident is that it didn't happen sooner.'* I repeat the line from the poem. I don't know how I remembered it, I think I was so enamoured that it locked in my brain.

'Groupie,' Gideon laughs.

'Show me?' I ask and he exhales loudly and rolls up his sleeves again. 'Oh. Gideon,' I sigh. They look so painful.

'Yeah,' he says. He doesn't look at his arms, just at me, looking at his arms. I run my fingers along some of the scars. There are small round ones. Perfectly round.

'What are these?'

'Burns.'

'Burns?'

'I had a lighter.'

This wash of, I don't know, shock and sad and bad. I just feel bad for him. Bad that he would do that to himself. I can't even imagine what that would feel like. I'm the biggest sook out so the idea of doing that to myself just, I don't get it.

'It's okay,' he says, and he rolls his sleeves down again.

'It's just. I feel really—' I don't know what to say to him. 'Why?'

Gideon shrugs. He stands up and walks over to his record player and he flicks the record over, puts the needle down and turns back to me. He waits until old R&B from the sixties plays, before looking at me. 'Everything felt too big. Too out of my control.'

'But not that?'

'No.' He pauses and comes and sits back next to me. 'It was pain on the outside that I could see, then watch it heal, you know?'

'Weren't you scared?' I ask.

'Um, yeah,' he stumbles, 'I didn't want to kill—' he stops himself and looks at the floor. 'Do. That.'

'Yeah.'

'But I just needed to feel some—yeah. Feel. Something other than. Petrified.'

'Then what?'

'When Suse saw. Um. We sat in the bathroom and we talked about it for ages. And her and Mum googled it. And I went and talked to a heap of people until I found someone I liked.'

I have this feeling of gratitude wash over me, feeling grateful that he's telling me any of this. I've never had anyone be this honest with me. Ever.

'His name is Robbie. He's how I got into poetry.'

I've never met anyone like Gideon, this honest poet with a record player and lesbian mums who's never got drunk or tried to touch my arse.

'And have you done it since?'

'Nuh.'

'Have you wanted to?'

'Um,' he pauses, thinking about it. 'No. The feeling doesn't go away. It just. I don't know. Gets smaller,

smaller than me, than the sum of my parts.'

'What does that mean?' I ask. I feel so dumb some-times because I don't know what shit like that means, and because he's smart. He says things I don't under-stand and he thinks before he speaks.

'It's small enough to imagine fitting it in a box,' he says.

'You do?'

'Yeah. And I put it in the box and keep it here.' Gideon puts his hands on my stomach, and I don't think about sucking in or if he can feel my fat rolls or if he cares because I'm so intrigued by him.

'Always,' he adds.

'It doesn't go away?'

'Nah. Just isn't everything.'

'Kelly's was—' and I stop myself before I go on. I haven't really talked about her with Gideon before. I haven't talked about her with anyone who didn't already know her or who didn't have some vested inter-est in my wellbeing. He's just been so honest to me, and I think I can trust him. 'I think Kel's was too big to put in a box.'

'Yeah.'

'Bigger than the sum of her parts,' I say, and he smiles.

'Yeah.'

That's all he says. No shitty advice, or *Oh Ava, I know how you feel* or anything, just *yeah*, and it's so… very refreshing.

'Why haven't you ever asked me about it?' I ask him

and Gideon shrugs, so I keep rambling. 'You can. It's okay. I think. I don't know. I don't know.'

Gideon takes a deep breath in. 'I suppose I didn't ask because I figured you'd tell me if you wanted to. I suppose I knew that you knew that I knew. That and it's none of my business. But, if you want me to ask you about it I will.'

I don't say anything. I try and process everything he's just said and try and think about what I want to tell him, if I want to tell him. I think I do. I really think I do. Gideon is the first to break the silence.

'I'd like to know how you are. Don't you think it's funny that we're programmed to always just say okay or fine or great when someone says How are you? We don't ever sway. I kind of hate that.' He pauses. 'So, Ava, how are you?'

'I'm fine thanks. How are you?' I reply, smiling. I feel nervous, really nervous, but okay. Gideon laughs so I continue. 'I don't even know, really.' Neither of us says anything for a really, really long time. So, I start at the beginning, because I've been told that's a very good place to start.

'Her name is Kelly. Kel. She is my best friend.'

'Forever?'

'Yeah. Actually.' I smile.

'My sister, Annie, she's my best friend.'

There's a pause before I speak.

'I've made some shit choices this year.'

'We're allowed to make shit choices.'

'Yeah,' I reply and now that I'm talking, like really

talking, all of these thoughts pop into my head and I find it hard to grab just one to start with, so we sit in silence until finally all of the thoughts come pouring out at once.

'You know what breaks my heart?'

'I've never had my heart broken.'

'The idea that she was that sad. That scared. That things were that dark. If she'd been in an accident or something I just think it'd be easier knowing that it was quick, but she made a choice, and she couldn't make choices at the best of times. But she did.'

'I used to get bullied in primary school. Like, some other kids made life really, really difficult; they hated me.'

'That's shit.' We sit in silence again. I just stare at him and he looks at the wall. I can't think of a single reason why anyone would hate Gideon. Not one. I put my hand on his arm. The fabric of his shirt is soft, he looks at my hand and I look at him looking at my hand. I've never been bullied, or had any reason before this year to feel sad, really. I wonder if that's why he cut his arms—if it was that bad. These thoughts keep pummelling at me one after the other until another just bursts out.

'There's stuff she knows about me that no one knows. That no one ever will now. I have no memories with her not in them.' I pause and ask, 'Have you ever been in love?'

He is quick to reply: 'No.'

I just nod. 'We sat on a trampoline when we were

like, eight, and she told me about sex. And Santa. In one conversation. She was amazing.' I think this is the first time I've talked about her and smiled.

'How did you become friends?'

'Preschool. My tooth fell out and she helped me find it. I dropped it under the bag racks. Then she made some boy trade us his cupcake for my apple. I couldn't eat the apple because of my tooth.'

'How did she do that?'

'Dunno. I think she scared him. She was amazing. We shared the cake.'

'She *was* scary.'

He catches me off guard. He knew her? He had an opinion about her? It makes me feel weird and defensive and like I should never have told him anything about her. He didn't know her. He's exactly like the rest of them. I was wrong.

My eyebrows furrow as I say, 'No she wasn't.'

'No. I mean, in an unattainable way. Confident. She was confident. That's like kryptonite to boys like me.'

I exhale and smile all at once. He's right. She was. And I guess to boys like Gideon she was scary, completely. I completely get that.

'You knew her?'

'Of her. Knew of her,' he says, smiling, and it makes me smile too—so wide that my face squishes and my brain fogs and I can't hear anything, just this wave of, I don't know, joy maybe. Just for a second.

'I can't even imagine what you're feeling,' Gideon mumbles.

'I don't even know how I'm feeling most of the time. It's like sad times everything, and there's this thumping in my ears.' I pause. All of the thoughts again, muddling into one. 'I don't know how to flirt,' I blurt and I can't believe I did.

Gideon kind of coughs and quickly fumbles, 'Is that what this is? Oh. No. Me either. I don't know.'

So I quickly try and change the subject with the first thing that comes to mind. 'I hate maths. Do you hate maths?'

'Yes,' he replies, but I keep talking.

'And I don't really know what I've done these last few months.' That's a complete lie, I do know what I've done. Lincoln. Beer. Telling people to get fucked and a whole lot of nothing, really, except crying and being pissed off.

'I think that's okay,' he says with his head leaning to one side as he looks at me.

'It scares me that our brains can haunt us from the inside, you know?'

'Yeah.' He smirks, the way you do when it's an inside joke. 'I know.'

'That you can be so loved and yet so lonely,' I say and he nods and my new thing of just saying what I'm thinking causes my mouth to open and this to fly out: 'I'm scared. Are you scared?'

'All the time.'

I pause. 'And you really never wanted to do what Kelly did?'

'Honestly?' Gideon bites his lip. 'A couple of times.'

'Why didn't you?'

'I don't know. It scared me too much, I suppose.' He pauses, thinking. I bite the inside of my cheek. *Why didn't it scare Kelly? Why wasn't she scared?*

'What did it feel like?' I ask.

Gideon thinks for a while before he stammers painfully, 'At that time, it felt like...the only option.' He nods once and I swallow hard, looking at the ceiling so I don't cry.

'Do you think that's what she thought?'

'I don't know, Ava.'

My heart is racing and I feel like that time Kelly and I tried speed. We stole one pill from Lincoln and halved it. I felt all out of control and jittery but completely present at the same time. It was so weird. It's the only time I did it and I'll never do it again because it freaked me out so much.

'Do you believe in God?' I'm looking at Gideon, who kind of shakes his head at me. *What must he think?* He must think I'm crazy.

'Not in the bible sense,' he says. 'I like the idea of believing in something.' He half-smiles.

'I think faith is weird. That kind of hope. I don't think I have that. Not now,' I say.

There's a really long silence. The record has stopped playing music and it's just making this whirring sound. Gideon stands up and lifts the needle. He puts the record back in its cardboard sleeve and then puts on something else, some lady, all slow and sad, with this deep voice.

I say the first thing that comes to mind.

'How did I not know you prior to now?'

He keeps looking at the record player. 'You wouldn't want to have known me prior to now,' he says.

'Same.'

'I don't know about that,' Gideon turns and looks at me. He jams his hands in his pockets and moves his foot around the carpet.

'Can you tell me another one of your poems?'

Gideon laughs; he doesn't look up, just keeps making swirls in the carpet. Rubbing them out and then starting again.

'Nope,' he says.

'Please?'

'No.'

'Why?'

'They're so bad.'

'I know that's not true now.'

He breathes deep. 'Okay. Close your eyes.'

'Why?'

''Cause I'm nervous.'

I smile and close my eyes. I can hear him moving. I peek under my eyelashes and see him pick up a note-book, flick through the pages. He's actually going to read one. I can hear him breathe in and almost with a whisper he starts.

I close my eyes. I want to listen, really listen.

a spectacle scene speckled with grief / she slammed into my sphere like a meteor / her debris lines my street / noticeable / unavoidable / she is unavoidable.

My throat tightens and my mouth feels really dry all of a sudden. I'm frozen and I keep my eyes shut tight.

> her heart is like shattered glass / I found her on her knees collecting it piece by piece to put it back together / but all she had was some clag and everyone knows that shit doesn't stick / but this girl / her voice is made of superglue it speaks and sticks and stays.

My chest, something is happening in my chest, this tightening, maybe because I hold my breath. I still don't open my eyes.

> she's got a dustpan mind right now / ready to throw it all away / she thinks it's too broken to fix / but everything is fixable with patience and care / get me a pair of those goggles with the light at the centre / i'll sit for hours and piece it together.

I swallow hard. The tears finally fall but I don't move as I watch Gideon read from the book. He's standing so still.

> it might not look the same when I'm done but at least–it will be hers / she is lost / and i can't claim to find her / i don't even know if she wants to be found / but i'll bend down beside her / help her pick up the shards.

He closes the notebook, slowly raising his head to look at me. I'm sobbing as I stand up, walk out the door, down the stairs, past his mums in the lounge room. They say something when they see me but I don't stop. I walk out the front door and I keep walking until I get home.

•

The last time Kelly was hospitalised she told me she just felt numb. She even said she'd prefer it if it hurt, or she was angry or sad, even; it was the nothingness that made her feel heavy.

'I just, I don't feel anything.' She was lying on her side on the hospital bed. Her mum and dad were talking to the doctors just outside the room. Visiting hours were limited to a couple of hours in the afternoon so I'd always come and just sit. I never knew what to say when she'd say things like this so I'd mostly just say nothing. Or nothing useful. I didn't want to fuck it up by saying the wrong things. Other times when I'd ask her questions about it she'd crack the shits big time or she'd quickly change the subject. I guess I'd just got used to saying nothing. I wish I hadn't.

'Do you want Twisties or salt and vinegar?' I asked, pulling my bag up onto my lap while Kelly just looked at me and shook her head. 'Bullshit, you never say no to chips,' I laughed.

'I'm not hungry,' she said.

I remember looking at her and just feeling this overwhelming sense of dread. This was different to the last times Kelly had an episode. She'd been hospitalised twice before. Once when we were in Year 9 but she was only in there for like a night and they just told her if she was feeling suicidal again that she had to tell an adult and then come back to the hospital. Which I thought was fucked because as if she was going to say anything. I hated that they made her so responsible for her own illness. Like it was all her fault. No one ever understood really. None of the doctors or the therapists. Not her parents. Not Lincoln or me. Not even Kelly.

'Promise me you'll say something,' I told her as we lay on her bed at her place the night after.

'Yeah, okay. Just stop talking about it,' she said, rolling her eyes.

The second time, which was earlier this year, they actually put her into a psych unit for a whole week. She'd get daily therapy. But she hated it there too. Everyone else there was older or sicker than she was and it made her feel worse. One afternoon when I visited her a really, really thin girl, like you could see her entire rib cage skinny, was crying and screaming. I had never seen anyone so thin, it was like her skin just hung off her bones, all limp. We stared at her as she pulled at her hair and banged on her chest and screamed at this nurse who did nothing, just watched her. She was screaming because the nurse was trying to feed her a Yogo.

'At least I'm not scared of Yogo,' Kelly smiled, and we giggled and felt bad for the anorexic girl.

So, the thing with the chips felt huge. She didn't want the chips. It was the moment when I realised how bad things actually were. For the first time I thought about the fact that one day she might actually succeed. That her parents wouldn't read the signs or they'd stop being overcautious or she'd stop asking for help. In that moment the size of that sadness was too big to even let into my brain. My throat clamped shut so I couldn't swallow and tears instantly welled, so I made myself think about something else. Those thoughts were like the sight of black clouds on a sunny day. And I just slammed the door so I couldn't see them anymore. But from that moment I could always hear the thunder. Knowing that something bad might happen.

But then she'd be okay. Things would go back to normal and we'd take the piss out of teachers, go to parties, sleep in each other's beds, get drunk and talk about how brilliant it would be when we were older.

I wish I could remember the specifics of the last time we hung out, the last time we talked. I've run it on repeat over and over again in my head to try and see if I missed any clues. But it was just a normal day. I can't even really remember what we talked about because it was that normal. We'd sat on the floor of my bedroom spiralling into a YouTube vortex of pimple-popping videos—clinging to cushions, squealing, unable to drag our eyes away. At one point that afternoon she'd been looking at my desk and picked up a framed photo of us from Year 7 camp where we're both sunburnt and freckly and wearing backwards caps. It was after I'd kissed Kyle Chong behind the girls' cabins in free time, my first kiss ever. Kelly had kissed his twin brother Jimmy. It was a dare. Kyle had braces and I could feel them clash into my teeth. We spent the night laughing because Jimmy had grabbed Kelly's boobs mid-pash, except he'd done it super quick.

'He just kind of honked my boobs,' Kels said, squinting her eyes, disgusted, while some other girls in our cabin and I howled with laughter. 'Like this,' and she demonstrated the quick double-handed grab he'd done on her boobs.

'What did you do?' one of the girls asked, wide-eyed.

'I pushed him away and just, like, walked off like this.' She folded her arms around her chest and stalked around the cabin with a repulsed look on her face. I was crying with laughter. We took the photo just after that.

'This is my favourite photo of us,' she said, holding the frame in her hands.

'Me too.'

'We look so happy,' she said. 'We're so stoked with ourselves.'

'That's because you'd just experienced sexual ecstasy with Jimmy Chong.' I started to giggle. 'Honk honk.' I mimicked the action in the air. Kelly didn't laugh.

'I'll never forget it,' she said, putting the frame back on the desk. Then she picked up a whiteboard marker and walked over to my mirror, rubbed out the dick she'd drawn a week before and replaced it with a love heart. She kept rubbing it out and starting again, making it perfect.

None of this was weird. She'd always draw or write things on the mirror. She'd always laugh about that photo. At the time I just thought it was a normal afternoon. Maybe it was for her too. But maybe it wasn't. Maybe she already knew what she was going to do, maybe that's why she said what she did and why she drew the love heart. She had wanted me to know that she'd never forget me and she loved me.

That night her mum picked her up, she had dinner with her family and said goodnight like she normally would. Then in her room she made some really shitty choices and drank a heap of vodka. She tucked herself into bed. She didn't write a note. She must have vomited in her sleep, because that's how she actually died. She choked.

I can't help thinking about her in her bed. Choking. What if she'd decided she didn't want to anymore? What if she tried to vomit it up but was too drowsy to lean over the side of the bed?

What if, in the end, she didn't want to die, but it was too late?

I've been thinking about Kelly all weekend, all the details of these moments, trying to find new information, trying to work out if things were for Kelly like they were for Gideon. Too much, too big. So huge that they consumed her and all she could feel was the pain. It must have been. If she really felt like it was her only option. She must've. Why else would she have done it?

I stayed at home all weekend trying to process everything. I don't know why I walked out. I don't know what I'm meant to say to him now. I'm so embarrassed. I feel like I need to apologise but I don't really know what for, or what I'd say.

That's when I notice the flash of mint green sitting on the kitchen bench amid a pile of junk mail. No stamp, just my name on the front. There's a card inside. It's homemade. On the front is a drawing of a penguin.

On the inside, it reads:

Ava,

I'm sorry.

Gideon

I feel awful. I bite my lip, my eyes sting. I keep thinking of him standing there reading the most beautiful
poem ever, basically saying that he wants to help me,
and I couldn't even say thank you. I don't know what's
wrong with me. I hate it. I hate feeling this way, feeling
like I will never, ever feel anything good, or normal or
like myself ever again. I'm so over it. I'm so over myself.
I wish I could take a break, just get away from my own
thoughts, from the stupid shit I keep doing. I wish I
could fix everything. I wish she never died. I wish she
told me how she felt. I'm angry with her. So, so angry.
Then I feel shit for being angry with her, because I love
her. And I would give anything to just hang out and talk
about nothing and tell her about this boy I've met who
wrote me a poem, an amazing, lovely poem. I'd tell her
that I freaked and walked out, and that I'm confused
and I don't know how to make it right, and that now he
thinks he did something wrong. Which he didn't, not
even a little bit. Everything he did was perfect.

He was right, I am broken.

•

Every Monday morning in English we spend the whole
lesson doing an exercise which Jason calls free writing.
We can write whatever we want as long as the pen

doesn't stop moving. Today I wrote a poem. A poem about Kelly. It just kind of poured out and I surprised myself with how easily it happened. I've never written a poem before. I have started a million diaries in my lifetime but I never stick to it; write one or two entries and then give up because I never know what to say.

You look like shit, I read scrawled on the piece of paper Minda just handed me in class. *I feel like shit,* I quickly write back and pass it to her. *You wanna talk about it?* she writes, glancing up to make sure that Jason doesn't see us. I shake my head.

Minutes later she taps my leg under the desk and points to her notebook: *what happened?* I think for a moment, and then write the words *I fucked up and I don't know how to fix it,* on my own page. Minda writes the words *A guy?* on her page and points at her notebook. I nod. *Just tell him how you feel.* I roll my eyes as she starts writing again.

NO BULLSHIT is written in giant capital letters in her book.

I think about this all day. About what I can tell him that would make sense to him. I begin three poorly constructed letters attempting to explain and apologise and convince him that me walking out had nothing to do with him or the poem and everything to do with me. But every single one of them is crap because I do a really shit job of explaining how I feel. My pen stops. I don't know what to say, but all of a sudden I know exactly what to do. I open my notebook to the pages

I wrote this morning, rip out the page with the poem on it, quickly scrawl a note and put it in an envelope. I walk straight around to Gideon's house and stuff it in his letterbox. If he wants to know what is in my brain. Well, that's exactly it.

GIDEON

'What else?' Robbie asks.

'I'm pissed off. I shouldn't feel this way,' I tell him. 'Things are pretty fucking great at the moment. I just shouldn't feel like—' I stop myself.

'What?' he asks.

'This. Sad. Not even sad. I feel. Out of it and angry. Really fucking mad.'

'At?'

'Myself. For feeling this way. Again.' I stare at Robbie. Today he is wearing a bright orange T-shirt with a picture of two cartoon oranges made to look like John Travolta and Samuel L. Jackson in *Pulp Fiction*. Pulp. Ha.

'Is it the same?' He looks down at his shirt and back at me, smiling.

'No and yes. I don't feel the same way. I don't

feel—' I breathe out. I hate these moments of having to describe what feels completely indescribable. Matching words to feelings is the worst fucking thing ever. That's the point, I'm feeling it, I don't want to talk about it.

But if I said that to Robbie he'd just smirk at me because he'd then say something like, 'You know.'

And I do. Talking about it is how I navigate it. Acknowledging what it is means there's strategies and if there's strategies there's forward momentum and if there's forward momentum there's wellness. That's all we're ever striving for. Wellness. Whatever that feels like.

'I don't feel,' I repeat myself, 'dark. It doesn't feel dark. It just feels flat. Like I can't think properly. Can't make decisions. Can't differentiate between what are my real thoughts and what are my thoughts because I feel...' I sigh, frustrated. 'Just everything feels foggy. Like a big fog.'

Robbie nods and asks, 'What else?'

'I feel disappointed in myself for being back here again.'

'Okay. But you are different. You are not the same Gideon dealing with your depression this time.'

'True.'

'It doesn't matter how small the changes, we are never the same as we were. It's important to have perspective.'

'I just wish it wasn't something I had to deal with.'

'I know. But you do.' He pauses. 'How did you feel when Ava left?'

'Like I'd fucked up, I shouldn't have read that poem.

We'd just had this really honest conversation and then I went too far.' I look at Robbie. 'I don't blame her for leaving.'

It feels good to talk about Ava with Robbie, a relief. But I also feel bad, like I'm betraying her trust or something. Like our conversation should be sacred and we should be the only two people in the world who know about it. Me and her. But now there's three—me, her and Robbie.

'And now I just feel—' I say.

'Bare?' Robbie asks. He'll do this, help me find the right words. I like it. His vocabulary is better than mine. And usually he's right.

'Yeah.'

'Vulnerable.'

'Yes. Completely. And that's really fucking scary, Robbie.' He nods and smiles. 'I don't want to upset her,' I tell him. It's true, I don't.

'I don't think you did.' Robbie looks at me and I raise my eyebrows, unsure. 'You didn't hurt her. You didn't *make* her cry. She cried because she had an emotional response to you, to your scars, because of her stuff.' He grabs his long hair and in two swift movements he ties it up in a bun with a rubber band at the crown of his head, revealing his undercut. I think what I like most about Robbie is that he genuinely doesn't care. He does what he wants and says what he wants when he wants. I wish I was more like that.

'How do you feel about her grief?'

'I don't feel anything about her grief,' I say quickly.

Robbie just as quickly laughs. 'Gideon, there are very few things that you don't feel anything about, mate.'

I laugh. 'I'm feeling definite things about your man bun.'

Robbie smirks. 'Are they feelings you want to talk about?'

I laugh at him. 'Not even a little bit.'

We smile at each other and Robbie raises his eyebrows, pressing for an answer. I don't know what to say.

I told Robbie about receiving her letter and poem and what it said.

> You have nothing to be sorry for. I don't know how to explain. I wrote a poem. I blame you. I've never written a poem before. Read it if you're confused about me. I just need you to know you did nothing wrong. It was all me and I think we should hang out again.
>
> Love Ava

I chose not to read the poem. Not yet. I don't feel confused about her. I don't know if she meant for me to take that literally, but I will, because that's what I do. I put it in my top drawer next to my bed and I'll read it when I'm confused. I don't know why. I wasn't confused when she just walked out on Friday night. As I thought back on every single detail of the night over and over again, the things we'd talked about, my two poems, my scars, our conversation, I realised it all must've brought up a lot of stuff for her about Kelly.

I don't know how to answer Robbie's question because I don't think I've really thought about Ava's grief as a thing. It's just part of her and I don't know her without it. I think she's sad and fragile…

'She's fragile. But also not. She's really, really strong. She's really amazing. I think I'm helping her.'

'Do you want to help her?' Robbie asks.

'Yeah. I do.'

'That's a responsibility.'

'Yeah. It is. But. I feel like I can.'

'Okay. Help?'

'Yes,' I tell him.

'Can she help you?'

'I don't want her to help me,' I say before I even realise.

'That seems a bit one-sided then.'

'I really like her.'

'*Like* like?' Robbie asks without a hint of sarcasm.

'Are you a fifteen-year-old girl?' I ask.

'If I had a dollar for every time someone said that to me,' he says.

I'm not really sure about many things at the moment, but how I feel about Ava, that's totally clear to me, even if I'm too scared to admit it.

'Yeah, I *like* like her,' I tell him. 'I, like, like her. A lot.' Robbie smiles. But I'm afraid it's not about whether I like, like Ava. The more important question is whether Ava like, likes me. Which I'm hand on heart one hundred per cent sure that she doesn't. I refuse to let something like my feelings ruin our friendship.

'Do you know what the Japanese say about broken things?' Robbie looks at me. '*Kintsukuroi* they call it. They take broken pieces of porcelain and they repair the cracks with gold. Making it as it was, but new again. They believe that the cracks can make something more beautiful, more valuable.'

'Is that for real?'

'Have I ever lied to you?'

'Never.'

'They believe that the cracks shouldn't be hidden, that they're part of their history, and should be shown. If you're going to show the cracks, why not show them beautifully.'

'So Ava's like a Japanese mug?'

'Yup, and so are you. We've all got cracks, Gideon.'

'Yeah.'

'Show her yours, if you want, cause they're part of you. They might help her. Help her, not fix her. It's not your job to fix her.'

I get it. I get the metaphor. There's no point pretending that everything is okay and that I'm not broken too. Because I am. I need to also realise that she's not a mug that I need to put back together or fix or be careful with. She's just Ava, and yes, she's got some pretty big cracks but they just make her more beautiful. She'd never have let me in like she has if I hadn't met her when I did. If I'd met her while Kelly was still alive she would've probably just fobbed me off. She didn't need me in her life then. But I think she needs me now.

'Well played, sir,' I say. 'How do I tell if she likes my cracks?'

'You gotta fill 'em with gold first, buddy boy,' says Robbie.

'Yes.'

'Shall we talk meds?'

'I don't want to change 'em.'

'Shall we talk strategies then?'

'Yup.' So we do. I leave my last session with Robbie for a while armed with a new notebook and some strategies.

•

'I'll tell you mine if you tell me yours,' Ava says, smiling.

Innuendo aside, I feel a normal wash of anxiety cool my system. Are we really going to do this? As far as people go I feel comfortable with Ava, but this feels unsafe. Or maybe this is just the way that everybody feels when there's someone insanely attractive lying on their bed expecting them to share their secrets.

We managed to get through three shifts together over the weekend at Magic Kebab with copious banter and giggling—righting the course of our friendship after the weirdness with the poem and Ava walking out. But maybe we're pushing our luck by spending tonight together, hanging out at my house. In my room. On my bed.

'You go first,' I mutter.

'Okay. But there has to be rules.' She sits up and crosses her legs.

'You're so bossy,' I smirk, knowing I'll get a reaction. She scoffs and hits me hard on the arm.

'I'm serious. Rule one, no commentary once someone has shared. Just say the thing and then that's it. You've said it. The other person knows. Done.' All her words smash together in quick succession. She's serious.

'Okay,' I nod.

'Okay, really? You promise to say nothing?' Her hands race forward and land on my leg, but just as quickly as they land, they're gone. She uses her hands to punctuate her sentences. I make a mental note to add this to the list of things I like about Ava.

'What about non-verbal communication?' I ask.

'No. Nothing.'

'But what about your epic fortune-telling eyebrows?'

She laughs loudly. You can always tell what Ava is thinking. I like this about her too.

'Okay, for the sake of my non-compliant eyebrows, non-verbal communication is fine.'

'I feel like we should shake on it,' I say, which we do. The anxiety morphs into excitement mixed with nerves, which I picture looking like erratic, colourful worms squiggling all around my body making my skin feel weird.

'Go then,' I say, watching her bite her teeth together and scrunch up her face, kind of pained. She breathes out quickly. 'I don't think I love my mum.'

When I open my mouth she promptly puts her hand over it, so I poke my tongue out and lick the palm of her hand and she pulls back, repulsed and laughing.

'Go,' she says.

I take a deep breath. 'You are the first girl I've ever had in my bedroom.'

Ava's head tilts and she takes a breath in preparation to speak but I shake my head. She smiles, and I watch her eyes dance all over my face.

The silence lasts a little too long so I whack her on the knee and she says, 'I once sneezed so hard I pooed my pants.'

The laughter erupts out of my mouth like an explosion, tears streaming down my face. I hold up five fingers as a hint for her to tell me how old she was.

'It was last week.' She pauses, and then she cracks up laughing. 'I'm kidding. I'm kidding.' She lies back on the bed, looking at the ceiling. 'I was in Grade 1. At school. My dad had to come pick me up.' She glances at me and I laugh more as I lie down on my side next to her.

'Annie once walked in on me masturbating,' I say. It was just before she left. I didn't think anyone was at home and I had my headphones in. It was completely horrifying for both of us and we've never ever talked about it.

Ava shakes her head. 'Your family really need to learn how to knock.' She gets it out quick while I put my finger to her mouth to 'shh' her and we fall apart giggling. Like, pain in my stomach, I can't breathe giggling.

Finally Ava sits up, leans all her weight on her elbows and looks at me seriously. 'That bruise,' she says, 'the one on my cheek that day? I wasn't dumb.' She pauses. 'Lincoln Waititi did that.'

She sits up and puts both her hands over my mouth so I really can't speak and she just stares at me and I stare at her. I cant believe she's kept this a secret.

I'm angry. She still talks to him. How dare he. He wanders around at school like a fucking macho dick-head and everyone fawns over him. I'm furious. I can feel my neck start to get really hot and I grab her hands from my mouth.

'You need to tell someone,' I say. Her wrists still in my hands.

'Shh. You promised.'

'But he's not—we're not meant to hit each other.'

'We got in a fight,' she says, shaking her head. 'It was an accident. I pushed him and he pushed me back and I fell and hit my face.' We don't say anything. I let go of her hands and she crosses her legs, facing away from me.

'He pushed you?' I mutter, staring at the back of her head.

'He didn't mean it.'

'He pushed you. He meant it.'

She doesn't say anything. This is massive. I don't know what I'm meant to say or what I'm meant to do.

Slowly Ava nods. 'Yeah.'

'And I'm the only one who knows?' I ask.

'Yeah.' She turns around to face me, but keeps her knees close to her chest. 'He's—' She pauses. 'Sad.'

'Fuck, Ava. What a dick. I'm so—' and she interrupts me.

'Don't.'

I just stare at her for a moment as she leans her chin on her knees. 'Are you okay?' I ask.

'No. Yes. I don't know, I'm not myself, I don't feel like myself,' she fires in one quick breath. 'Your turn.'

I take a really deep breath. I'm assuming that's her biggest secret. It's only fair for me to tell her mine. 'We moved because of me.'

'Why?'

'Because I wasn't okay.' She unfolds her hands and crosses her legs, watching me, 'All through school I got picked on. Because I was tall or cause my mums were gay or my sister was smart. In Year 7, I got really sad and I wrote this story about a sad moon during an eclipse and some kids found it, copied it and stuck it up all over the school. It was just small things. Stupid shit. But lots of stupid shit. All of the time.'

'That's really awful. I didn't—'

I cut her off. If I'm going to tell her, I'm going to tell her all of it. 'They made a website.'

'What?' she asks.

'Www dot we hate Gideon dot com filled with all this hateful shit. They'd take secret photos of me at school and post comments and—'

'Oh, Gideon, that's so fucked.' She puts her hand on my knee, only this time she doesn't move it.

'Yeah.'

'What happened?'

'It all blew up. My parents were furious and so they went to town on the school. They found out it was this one group of kids doing it all. Their parents dug in and said it was all just fun, which only made my parents even crazier and the school handled it really badly. Then one night someone spray-painted the words *fag house* on our garage.' I pause because Ava has her hand over her mouth, mortified. 'The next day Annie took a baseball bat to school and fully raged out.'

Ava starts to giggle but quickly stops herself. 'I'm sorry.'

'It's okay. That part is funny now. She was so angry she knocked out one of the kids' teeth. Their parents wanted to sue. So we moved.'

Ava says nothing but I can see on her face that she's trying to process what I've just said.

'I keep a lot of stuff in.'

'No shit,' she says. 'But your poems?'

'That's not me. Or it is. But that feels like a different person. Kind of.' I pause. Ava doesn't say anything. 'It's just my brain—I get real bad anxiety. And I'm a bit—'

She cuts me off, nodding slowly. 'Yeah.'

But I keep going: 'And I'm in a bit of dark moment right now, but it's okay. I'm on medication.'

'Okay.'

'It's just—my brain.'

'Is like Kelly's brain.'

'I guess.' I lie down on my side, and Ava doesn't move. I listen to us both breathing. Eventually she crawls over and lies down facing me so we're lying nose to nose.

AVA

After a while I speak. 'Gideon, I think you're amazing.'

He closes his eyes. I see him swallow. Then a single tear runs down his cheek. Three quick, sharp intakes of breath and then that's it. He just sobs, large, heavy, painful sobs. He rolls over away from me and cries into the pillow. I put my arm under his and rest it on his chest and I hug him. I'm the big spoon. I hug him hard. I can feel his whole body heaving as he tries to catch his breath between his sobs. Neither of us says anything. We just lie there. Then he moves and he places his hand on mine, pulling it closer into him, tucking it right in at the middle of his chest, and intertwines his fingers with mine.

'I'm sorry,' he finally says.

'Don't—'

He cuts me off. 'No. I'm sorry, you don't need to deal with my shit—'

'You've been dealing with mine,' I say, and it's true.

'Yeah, but—'

I cut him off. 'I just think that maybe we're meant to.'

'What?'

'Deal with each other's shit,' I say.

'You and me?' Gideon asks.

We lie there squished so closely together and we talk in whispers.

'No. Everyone,' I murmur.

Gideon rolls over so he's flat on his back. He doesn't let go of my hand and he doesn't look at me.

'There's so many people around me who don't let me help them,' I say. 'My dad, Lincoln. Even Kelly. She'd tell me it was a bad day *after* her bad days, you know? I'd get a text to say her parents had taken her to hospital again or I'd just wake up and she'd be in my bed because she'd run away again. Or she'd go silent and I wouldn't hear from her or she'd just send me sad-face emojis. But we never really talked about it. Not really.'

Gideon takes a deep breath; I can tell he's thinking about what to say. 'She probably didn't want to worry you.'

'I wish she had. There was this whole part of her life, this whole part of her brain, that I didn't know about. I just think that maybe—'

'You can't do anything, Ava.' He knows what I was going to say. How does he do that?

'You don't know that.' There has to have been

something that I could've done, even something small. There has to have been.

'Yeah, I do,' he says. And of all people he does know. 'There's nothing you can do.' He turns his head and looks at me. His eyes are still glazed but they look a different colour, a lighter brown maybe. Like the tears have washed some of the colour away.

I try to pull my hand away but he holds my wrist with both his hands and runs his fingers over mine, like he's studying them.

'Except this. You can do this,' he says. 'Be here.'

I can't help it, the valve between my thoughts and tears is so worn down that I don't think I have any control over them anymore. Fat tears drop onto my cheeks. I feel them before I even know what's happening and I just let them fall. I pull my hand and Gideon rolls over to face me.

'Hey? Hey, what's—?' he says, looking at me.

'You.'

'I don't want to—'

'You,' I interrupt. 'You being sad. I just hate that. I hate that your brain does that to you.'

'I don't want to make you cry. Ever.'

'I just—'

'Yeah. I know. I know, Ava,' he whispers.

I believe him. Sometimes I think he knows more about how I feel than I even do.

'I hate that there's nothing I can do,' I sob.

'Ava.' He pauses and just watches me try to catch my breath. 'I'm not going anywhere.'

He says this with complete certainty.

I nod and I cry and he wraps his arm around me and he squeezes me and I cry. I cry because I don't want him to go anywhere and I'm so desperately worried about anything happening to him and I want to believe him. I want to believe that he's telling the truth. I cry because while I feel all of these things for him, a part of me still wishes he was her.

'Hey. Hey? Look at me,' Gideon says as he tucks my hair behind my ear and traces my jaw with his thumb until he gets to my chin. With his finger and thumb he lifts my face. So gently. I don't say anything. He wipes my cheek with his thumb, drawing a half-circle on my cheek.

'Hey, I have to ask you something?'

'What?' I mutter.

'Are you getting snot all over my pillow?'

My face cracks a smile and I wipe my nose with the back of my hand.

Gideon sits up and clambers over and I can hear his steps on the wooden floorboards as he dashes to the bathroom. He returns ten seconds later with a toilet roll, throws it at me and sits on the edge of the bed near my feet.

I sit up and blow my nose and watch Gideon. He's looking at the floor, his elbows leaning on his knees and his hands lined up perfectly. I wish I could read his mind.

•

'Ava, are you going out tonight?' Dad asks.

I shake my head and he looks genuinely surprised. 'Well, do you want to do something?' He pauses. 'Hang out?' This dorky smile cracks his face and it makes me laugh.

'Yeah.'

After an intense conversation about our options we settle on staying in and watching a movie. We compromise. I'll choose what we're eating and Dad chooses the movie. We'll end up watching some shit action thing with a war because he loves them, but I don't care, he seems genuinely excited to spend time with me.

Dad walks in with pizza and a plastic bag filled with confectionery and throws me a mint envelope.

'Who keeps sending you letters?'

'Gideon.'

'The poet?'

'Yeah.'

'That's very romantic,' Dad smiles, and I scoff, shaking my head. I can feel my cheeks flush.

'We're just friends.' He doesn't look convinced. 'He doesn't have a phone...or the internet. So we write letters. It's very innocent.' Dad mutters something to himself as he walks into the kitchen and I throw a cushion at him.

I open the envelope and an A4 page with the words *Make Magic* in big biro bubble letters takes up the whole thing with a tiny weird sketch of Ricky's kangaroo tattoo at the bottom. The drawing is so bad. I crack up laughing. There's a tiny ripped note and all it says is:

History was boring today so I made you this.

P.S. Kangaroos are hard to draw.

Dad walks back into the living room staring at me with this weird look. 'What?' I say.

'Nothing.' He smiles. 'I want to meet him.'

'I think you'll like him. He's very…' I try to find the right word. 'Different. He's cool. He makes me laugh.'

'I can see that.' I tell him about Ricky's tattoo and he looks repulsed. 'That's disgusting. Why would he send that to you? You don't need a reminder of that on your wall.' He smiles.

'He's a good guy, Dad.' I pause. 'He's been a really good friend.' And I stuff a piece of pizza in my mouth in the same way that I stuff down any thoughts that Gideon could be anything else.

GIDEON

Another boring day at school. Another boring lecture about the future. I can't decide—is it so tedious lately because we're close to the end and I'm just over it? Or is something else going on?

I've had a plan about my future since Year 9. Do well. Get into uni. Study writing. Move away. Start my life. Be happy. Simple. It's always been my lifeline when things were shit, this miraculous concept that one day it would stop being shit because I wouldn't have to go to school anymore and I could do what I wanted, where I wanted and hell, I'd even get to be the kind of guy I wanted to be. It was going to be so awesome. But now it's actually right around the corner, so close I can see it, I don't find it as exciting anymore. I think I'm terrified. What if the plan doesn't work? Worse still, what if I change my mind?

There's a letter from Ava on the kitchen bench when I get home. I rip it open and a small sketch of a kangaroo floats to the floor with the words: *better than yours*. I laugh. It is better than mine.

Gideon,

It's just after midnight and I can't sleep so I thought I would write you a letter. If you were a normal person with a phone I would've sent you a photo of me pulling a stupid face, hoping you'd be awake. If you were awake you would reply and then we could talk about stupid shit until I finally felt tired. But you don't, so now I just need to talk to myself knowing that you'll read it. Letters are weird.

We've been looking at memoirs in English and we have to write this personal reflective essay about a life lesson we've learnt and want to share. I had been finding it really fucking tricky to decide what I wanted to write about but your picture helped me decide. I'm going to write about Ricky, about his dickhead policy and about, well, making your life magic. I feel like that's one life lesson I can write about. So thank you for your help...in more ways than one. Like this weekend for example, thank you for that in advance, you're a good guy, Gideon. Like, really. I even said that to my dad. He wants to meet you, by the way...he called you a renaissance man. I don't know what that means. I hope it isn't a bad thing.

Love Ava

I smile and feel the weird flip that my stomach does when anything to do with Ava Spirini occurs. I would never tell Ava how I felt about her. I would never want to ruin it. Besides, there is no chance that a girl like her would even slightly be interested in a guy like me. We are friends and that's how it is going to stay. I am well practised at ignoring my feelings. Robbie would agree: telling Ava how I feel about her is not a safe risk. No one wins. I'd put her in a position where she'd have to awkwardly tell me she *likes me as a friend* and then there'd be no chance of ever getting back to the way things are now. And I like things the way they are now. I like being Ava's friend. When I see her tomorrow she's going to need me to be her friend.

Tomorrow is Kelly's birthday.

Her plan had been to ignore it, but I convinced her to hang out, that I could help. If only by making sure she wasn't on her own. My plan is to buy an enormous assortment of ridiculous snacks. I've selected a range of movies that are not about death or suicide or best friends, which was more difficult than I thought it would be. And I have prepared another list of light-hearted topics in case things start to head into murky territory.

Tomorrow I'm going to be the best goddamn friend she's ever had.

AVA

Gideon and I are giggling about something stupid in the movie when there's a knock at the door and I pause the TV. I took a bit of convincing to hang out with him today; I had planned on sleeping all day and waiting for it to be over. Then I thought if I was going to feel like shit, I may as well do it with Gideon.

I throw a handful of Skittles at him as I trudge to the door and whip it open and Lincoln is standing there with a can of rum and Coke in his hand. I swallow hard; it's not even midday.

'What do you want?'

'To see you.'

'Why?'

'You know why.' He's unsteady on his feet and he clutches at the door frame.

'You haven't said anything to me in weeks and then

you just show up and think that everything will be back to normal? Go home, Lincoln.' I begin to shut the door but he pushes it back open.

'I thought we could hang out,' he slurs and takes a step past me into the house.

'I don't want to hang out.'

Gideon stands up from the couch. Lincoln looks at him and snorts. 'What, so you get a new boyfriend—'

'He's a friend,' I spit, 'and it's none of your business.'

Lincoln is seething. I don't care, I'm so mad at him. Gideon is frozen.

'It's her birthday.' My words sit heavy in the air.

Lincoln turns to face me. 'Special day, yeah? I thought we could celebrate.' He grabs my face with both his hands and kisses me hard on the mouth and I push him away with all of my strength. He looks at me, stunned, as I push him towards the door once again: 'I don't want to celebrate her birthday with *you*.'

He steps onto the porch and throws the can in his hand—hard—and it bounces on the concrete and lands with a heavy spray on the road as I slam the door.

'Fuck you, Ava,' he shouts.

Gideon strides towards me. 'Are you all right?'

'No.' I start pacing. 'I'm so angry. He hasn't talked to me in weeks since...the thing he did, and what? He thinks I'll just let him in and hook up with him like nothing happened?' Gideon makes a weird sound, but I keep rambling. 'He just doesn't listen. He doesn't think. He just gets shit-faced and acts like a jerk.'

'He is a jerk.' Gideon shakes his head.

'But he's not. He's just. We feel the same way.' My voice is strained and the tears sit in my eyes—ready to spill, just not quite yet. 'I wish you could've met her. Properly'—then they start—'and I wish you could've met me then too, because I feel like when she died, I died too. Or a bit of me did. My heart, maybe.'

Gideon hugs me tight, he lets me cry and he doesn't say anything. It's just all too heavy, like a dead weight on my chest. Like my throat is closing up and I can't breathe.

Lately I've been caught out by these moments where things are…good. Great, even. When I am happy with this hilarious boy who writes poetry and makes me laugh. And just as quickly as I feel good, I'll remember or I'll think of her, think that this is something I should tell her because she'd love it. All of it. She would've laughed her mad cackle and said something like 'I love this shit,' getting all giddy. She'd have wanted to know every single detail and she'd want me to repeat them over and over. I pull away and look at Gideon and he looks back at me with his floppy hair, expecting something and nothing all at the same time, and I'm petrified.

'Like you said, I'm broken. My heart. Is broken. So any of this. With you. Is just—' I stop. I hate myself. I hate what I'm saying even as it leaves my mouth.

Kelly would've yelled at me about sabotage, and told me to grow a set. Just go for it, like she would have done. Well, in her up moments she would. Her good days.

Then we'd have to work out plans upon plans to get her out of the situations she got herself into—like the time she wrote Andre Daar a love letter.

We were in Year 8 and Andre was in Year 12. He hadn't been in Australia long, a year maybe. He was from Somalia and didn't speak much English, but he beatboxed so all the kids at school thought he was cool. He was amazing. Is amazing. He's been signed to some label and works with big musicians now. Kel used Google translate to write a letter in Arabic and on Friday afternoon she put it in his locker. By Sunday night I was standing at school in one of Lincoln's hoodies holding a crowbar and a pair of tin snips because we had to get the letter back, which we did. No one ever found out it was us who'd busted Andre's locker open. Mrs Bryan did a big rant at assembly about equality and multicul-turalism, so everyone was led to believe that the great act of locker vandalism was in the name of hatred. No one ever found out it was actually in the name of love. Misguided love, but still.

Andre never knew that there were two girls in Year 8 who learned to say *I love you* in Arabic just for him.

Kel learned it just for him; I learned it because she made me.

'So, yeah. Gideon, I just—' and he interrupts me.

'Do you know what the Japanese do with broken things?'

I don't say anything.

'They put them back together. But they fill the gaps

with gold. They reckon the breaks are just a part of their story. That the cracks should make the piece more beautiful.'

I pause. 'You can't fix it, Gideon.'

'I know.'

And I can't fix it either. Because every time I think about the fact that she's not coming back my heart breaks again, and I hate this melodramatic shit so much. I read the blogs and the forums online and I see myself in all of them. They tell me it's normal. They say that time heals all wounds. But that's bullshit, it's just a stupid saying.

Time heals *some* wounds. Other wounds are too big. Some wounds kill you. Sometimes you don't even have a wound. Sometimes it's just your blood, or your brain, or your chemicals that make you sick. And sometimes your blood or your brain or your chemicals, or whatever it is kills you.

I look at Gideon. 'Sometimes I think. I don't want to kill myself, but if I died. That would be okay.'

'Ava.' He sits on the floor next to me.

'No. That would make all of this okay because I wouldn't have to feel like this anymore.'

Neither of us says anything, he just stares at me.

'Gideon. I'm so tired. I hate crying. I don't want to cry anymore. And you are so. Weird and—'

'Attractive?' He says this so fast that I half-smile through my snotty tears.

'Awesome. Kel would've fucking loved you. She would. She does, probably, I don't know. I hate that past-tense shit. God. I don't even know what to say when I talk about her.'

'I don't know what to say most of the time. No one I love has ever died.'

'Well, it sucks balls.'

'Yeah, I gathered. But maybe it gets lighter?' He grabs a handful of Skittles off the ground and starts making patterns with them.

'What?'

'The weight. It doesn't go away. But maybe you just work out how to carry it.'

'Like the box?'

'Like the box.'

He's made an 'A' out of the Skittles on the carpet. He doesn't look at me, just at the Skittles. I feel better. Slightly mystified. But better.

'Should we write a poem now?' I joke.

'We can.' Gideon looks at me and smiles. 'Roses are red. Violets are blue. Gideon thinks Ava is pretty... sometimes,' he says, holding my gaze for like a tiny moment before looking back down to the carpet.

'That's it?' I giggle through my nose, as my stomach tenses. 'That was awful.'

'I told you.'

'It didn't even rhyme.'

Gideon laughs loudly and I look up; take a big deep breath in. 'You're a good friend, Gideon.'

'Yeah.' He nods with a little tight smile.

'Do you know what the Japanese do with good friends?' I say.

Gideon laughs again. 'No, do you?'

I nod and I kiss him. I kiss him because I've never wanted to kiss anyone more than I want to kiss Gideon right now and he kisses me back and it just keeps going. It's the best kiss I've ever had. That is until a car horn beeps and Gideon breaks away and looks out the window. It's his mums. His face flushes bright red and he gets up and walks out the door to the car without saying anything at all. Just gets in the car and they drive off.

What just happened?

We kiss and he doesn't say anything. Was he embarrassed? Maybe he didn't want to, maybe his mums pulling up was the best thing ever so he didn't have to untangle himself and let me down gently. But I am no stranger to unwelcome kisses, and it definitely did not feel like that…It's like he'll let me in, then close up, and then I'll let him in and I'll run away. I just wish I knew how he felt.

I stand up and that's when I see it, on the carpet. Gideon's feelings written in Skittles.

G 4 A.

GIDEON

The same few thoughts have been running through my head on a loop. Ava kissed me. I kissed her back. *Ava and I kissed*. It was awesome. But then another series of thoughts run on repeat. You ruined it. You're a fucking idiot. Why did you walk out like that? What kind of crazy person kisses the person they like and then just... leaves?

That would be me.

I pace around my bedroom trying to work out my next move, trying to work out how to fix it, but I don't know what to do, so I call the only person who can help.

'So,' says Annie, 'tell me about this girl.'

So I do. I tell her about Ava. I tell her all about Ava, because I've attempted to maintain some kind of cool with everyone else, but there is nothing cool about me around Annie. She knows I had my very own My Little Pony collection when I was seven so I could play with her and her friends. She knows that I cried hysterically in the movie *All Dogs Go to Heaven*. I was twelve. She knows about the time I vomited all over myself going around a roundabout. Annie already knows I'm just incredibly uncool, so, I gush like an idiot. I tell her all about Magic Kebab, and our letters, and our kiss. I probably spend a good five minutes on things that Ava finds funny and the way she laughs and I tell Annie about the way she makes me feel: 'Like my stomach is going to twist itself up so tight with giddiness that it's going to fall out of my belly button.'

'Wow. Have you told her these things?' Annie smiles after I finish another longwinded rant.

'Well, no. Not really. She knows. She'd know, yeah?' I ask.

'Probably not.'

'So, I should tell her?'

'Absolutely. We all deserve to be fawned over, Gids. Tell her and don't walk out again. Stick around for the good bits.'

This induces nothing but a wash of fear. I thought this fear would go away once Ava and I kissed, but it hasn't. Is this what relationships are? Just a perpetual sense of dread? Why don't they talk about this in the romantic movies?

'Stop thinking about it, and just tell her,' Annie says. 'What's the worst thing that could happen?'

I think about all of the bad things that could happen.

That list is actually quite easy to imagine.

Annie continues, 'The worst is that she doesn't feel the same way. Yeah, that'll bruise, but so what? Is it going to change the way you feel about her?'

'No,' I say.

'Then do it.'

We pause. 'Okay, that's your heart. Now tell me about your brain,' Annie rests the iPad on her knees as she puts her hair up into a high ponytail on the top of her head.

'It's getting better.'

'You sure?'

'Yeah. Things are. Not like the last times, Annie. It's different. It's still...' I try to find the right word. 'It's still shit.'

'How poetic,' Annie laughs.

'Shut up,' I say, smiling at her, 'I'm okay. Just—' I stop myself.

'What?'

'Nah. It's nothing.'

'Tell me.'

It takes a while to get it out. Mainly cause I don't really know what I'm trying to say. I tell her that school is so pointless and that all of my uni applications are in, but when I think about next year now, I just feel totally numb. I used to think of moving and studying as the way out. As when my life would begin. I'd put so much emphasis on just getting through Year 12, on getting into uni, that now it's happening and it's so close, it just doesn't feel urgent anymore. It doesn't feel exciting. It just feels...nothing. Which completely freaks me out because what if it's not what I want? What if there is nothing to be excited about or look forward to anymore and what if this is the way I'm going to feel about things for the rest of my life?

'So, don't go to uni,' Annie says, matter-of-fact. 'If it doesn't feel right, don't go.'

I scoff at her. 'And do what? Work at Magic Kebab?'

'No.' She pauses. 'Come here.'

'For a holiday?'

'Maybe. Or come and live here. With me.'

I just look at her, feeling my forehead crease. 'You're not serious. I can't.'

'Why?'

'Because. Ava. And—' I stop, I can't think of any other reasons.

'That's it. That's your only reason?'

This is classic Annie. She's too smart to fight her corner, she just asks well-timed questions in the hope that you'll work it out for yourself.

'Come and have an adventure, Gids. Work out what you want. Write. Meet crazy people. See things. Feel some things.'

I don't say anything, and in an instant Robbie pops into my head. 'Fill your cracks, kiddo.' What a completely crazy idea. What would Ava say? She'd hate it. My mums would hate it. I couldn't...

'Just think about it. Okay?'

'Okay.'

'Now, aren't you gonna ask me about me?' She moves

189

the iPad to show me some guy with a big beard sound asleep next to her.

'Annie!' I yell, totally grossed out. 'Has he been there the whole time?'

'Gideon, meet Mario,' she smirks. 'He's Italian.'

I start laughing. 'Is he your boyfriend?'

Annie pokes at the bearded man and he opens one eye. 'Good morning beautiful,' he says with a thick accent while my eyes bulge out of my head. I can feel my cheeks flush, I'm so embarrassed.

'My brother wants to know if you're my boyfriend.'

Mario registers the iPad in her hands and makes eye contact with me. I probably should smile, I guess. Or maybe wave. I don't know. What's the polite thing to do when you meet the Italian man in your sister's bed? Mario takes the iPad out of Annie's hands, still lying down, and holds it directly above his face.

'Hello, Gideon, lovely to meet you, I've heard lots about your poems.'

He has? What has Annie told him?

'The one about the dandelion is my favourite.'

I wrote that for Annie before she left.

'Now, to answer your question.' He is smirking, but I can only tell because his beard moves. 'I am most definitely not Annie's boyfriend.'

I hear Annie scoff and she reappears in the screen with her head on his chest.

'There, that clears that up.' She pauses. 'I miss you, Gideon.'

'I miss you too.'

Then she hangs up. I don't want to think about what happens after that.

•

'You look hilarious,' Ava giggles. We're both wearing giant jackets and gloves. Today is the day we have to clean out the Magic Kebab cold room for Ricky. Today is also the first time we've seen each other since we kissed. The air between us is awkward.

'Does it suit me?' I say, posing with one hand on the shelf. My jacket is way too small and only comes down to my hips—I'm pretty sure it's a ladies jacket, whereas the same jacket on Ava covers her knees. She pulls the hood up and I crack up laughing. 'That's a good look. Yes.'

'You can't even see my face.'

'Exactly,' I say.

Thanks Ricky, I think, because these stupid, cheapskate jackets have definitely, pardon the pun, broken the ice between us.

We get back to checking use-by dates and throwing stuff away. A collection of the olive tins are six years out of date, which for some reason we think is hilarious. Then we find something in the back corner behind a box of meat that can only be described as alien. I've never seen anything with so many shades of mould on it.

'I'm not touching it.' Ava stands against the door as far as physically possible from the weird mouldy thing on the ground.

I poke it with a bit of cardboard. What is it, even?

'This is so gross,' she laughs as I grab a rubbish bag from my back pocket and move with feline grace to pick up the alien with the bag, flip it inside out and tie a knot in it. I turn to Ava and bow.

'I am like a freaking knight in shining armour,' I say, then do what any boy in my position would do and throw the bag at her. She screams and whacks it back at me and the weird black plastic mould mound sits on the floor between us. Who will make the first move in the great cold-room battle? Ava laughs nervously as I lunge for the bag and pick it up one-handed.

'Don't. Don't. Don't. Don't,' she squeals.

'Okay, okay. I won't.'

'Promise?'

'Yes. I am a man of my word.' I bend down and put the bag inside the giant bin we're using and feel a large whack on my head. Soggy bits of lettuce start to slide down my face as Ava jolts past, laughing wildly.

'What are you going to do now?' She looks around the cold room; she has backed herself into the far corner and has nowhere to go. She pleads wildly for forgiveness as I take two strides towards her and stuff another clump of lettuce into the hood of her jacket and pull it up over her head. She looks up at me. We both stop.

This is the closest we've been since the kiss. Ava pushes me up against the metal shelf and my heart starts to thud in my chest, she looks into my eyes with a kind of wry smirk. Leans up and kisses me.

I kiss her back and notice the squeak of our plastic

jackets colliding and oh my god I feel Ava's hand on the button of my jeans. I stop kissing her to breathe in deep. I can feel the cold metal on my back but I don't care—this is the hottest thing ever. I kiss her again as she pulls at the waistband of my jeans and her hand slides in and I'm trying desperately to keep my cool but then all of a sudden it is cool.

Cold, even. Cold and soggy—as Ava has just dropped a handful of lettuce into my pants.

AVA

I am completely pissing myself as I watch Gideon try to get the lettuce out of his jeans.

'You are vicious! A vicious, depraved human being, Ava Spirini,' he says, pointing at me. When I first got to work today, I was worried because things between us were so awkward. He couldn't look me in the eye and I thought—he regrets it, for sure. But when we got into the cold room the awkwardness eased and we had a laugh and found our old rhythm. He's a really good kisser. Like really good—I really, really like kissing him.

'There is definitely still lettuce in my pants,' he says, itching his legs, 'it feels like slugs.'

'Take them off then,' I say and Gideon looks shocked.

'I've heard about girls like you,' he says.

'Girls like me?'

'Yes. Girls who lure unsuspecting boys into small cold spaces to take advantage of them. Well, my mothers raised me right, and I will not be another one of your conquests, Ms Spirini. I've got morals.' He sits on a crate and starts to undo his boots.

I pretend to focus on the arrangement of the tins on the bottom shelf but I'm watching out of the corner of my eye as Gideon wriggles out of his skinny jeans and lettuce falls to the floor. Lined up the side of his thigh, just like his arms, are the same thin scars. Not as many, but they march up his leg with meticulous precision. I can't help it, I reach over and touch them as Gideon looks down at me with his pants in his hand.

'I forget they're there,' he says. He doesn't move. 'They're really ugly aren't they?' I look up at him and shake my head and touch the tiny scars one by one.

'I don't think you're ugly anywhere,' I tell him and he puts his hand on top of mine.

As he does the giant door to the cold room opens and there's Ricky, stunned in the doorway. Me on my knees and Gideon in his jocks, holding his pants in his hands.

Gideon is mortified. 'We can explain,' he stutters quickly, pulling on his jeans, but I just sit, smiling, because he's wrong, I can't explain what I'm feeling right now.

•

'Ava, I'm Nola.' She smiles. 'Don't worry, I'm not going to make you say or do anything that you don't want to do. You're paying me to help you out, and I want you to remember that. Because I think people get really freaked out about therapy and it's unnecessary. I like to remind all of my clients of this. I don't know you. I don't know any of the people you know. Everything I learn about you will come from you. You can tell me as much or as little as you like. But the idea is for me to help you work out a way to feel better. To come up with some strategies to be able to deal with whatever feelings you're having that you don't like. Does that make sense?'

Nola is calm. And beautiful. She has bright red lipstick that matches her bright red square glasses. I think she's probably in her thirties. She has a big diamond wedding ring. Her skin is a dark caramel brown and she has this thick Australian twang. She's quiet. She doesn't stare at me. Everyone at TAPs sees Nola if they want to. Minda said she was awesome and told me that I was an idiot if I didn't make an appointment.

'Do you want to tell me about you?' she asks.

'I don't really like talking,' I say, looking around her tiny office. There's a heap of kids' drawings in frames on the wall and a bookshelf that's jam-packed with books. She has a giant spray-painted mural hanging on a canvas on the wall, all swirls of oranges, blues and purples.

'About yourself or in general?'

'Both.'

'Okay. We don't have to talk. How do you feel about drawing?'

'I'm not very good.'

'It doesn't matter. How about I put some music on and we just draw and then we'll have something to talk about other than you?'

'Sure.' I figure I don't have anything to lose and anything that will avoid me having to talk sounds great to me.

I've been to one other therapist and two counsellors—they were all fine, asked the same questions, but they kind of talked to me like I was a child and it just pissed me off. I didn't go back to any of them, even though Dad wanted me to.

Nola stands up and walks over to a chest of drawers in the corner of the room. She opens the bottom drawer and pulls out two shoeboxes filled with craft supplies.

'Do you want to choose a song?' She says motioning towards the bookshelf where there's a stereo and an iPod. I walk over and start flicking through the artists and click play on Jeff Buckley.

Nola closes her eyes and nods. 'Good choice. I got this album when I was your age. It was very important to me.'

'I've only just started listening to it.' I pause. Gideon *made* me listen to it last week. 'My friend gave it to me.'

'Well, your friend has very good taste.' Nola kicks her shoes off and sits on the floor at the coffee table. I sit on the opposite side of her; spread out are coloured papers and jars of pens, boxes of pastels and crayons, glue sticks and other craft supplies and there's an empty art book placed in front of me.

'Now the idea of this is to just do whatever. Don't think about it too much. It can be scribbles or words or anything, really. Just go with whatever feels good.'

I smile at the obvious dirty innuendo and Nola's eyes glint a bit as she smiles. 'We don't do it enough.'

She opens her own art journal and grabs a yellow crayon and she starts drawing. I watch her for a moment as she swaps to a red crayon and makes large swirls, the crayon in her hand swishing around the page messily. Then I grab a black felt pen and start drawing squares.

A small square and then another square, and then another. I pick up a purple texta and draw a heart in the smallest box. I colour it in. Jeff Buckley's singing about goodbyes. A lyric catches my ear so I write it down in little letters at the bottom of the page, only I replace the word 'him' with the word 'her'. Grabbing three pastels in my hand at the same time I write it over and over again, bigger and bigger and bigger until that's all you can see, just big messy letters covering the whole page.

After a while Nola turns the music down and looks at my drawing.

'I don't even know what it is,' I say. I feel incredibly self-conscious.

'It doesn't have to be anything.' She looks at the picture and I watch her face to see if she's doing some kind of mad psychologist voodoo and is going to turn around tell me I'm a head case.

'If you were looking at this for the first time, if this was my picture, what would you want to know about first? Where do you reckon your eye would be drawn?'

'The heart,' I tell her.

'Yeah, okay. Why is that?'

'You can only just make it out. Only just notice it.'

'It's pretty small. Pretty well hidden,' she says.

'Yeah, it's covered by all of the other lines.' I don't know if this is right, if this is what she wants me to say, but it must be, because then we talk about the colours, the lines, the other things we both notice. The picture stops becoming something that I even drew and just becomes a thing we're talking about, until eventually I'm telling her about myself. About some of the things that have happened.

'I'm going to tell you exactly what I know about grief and it might make some things clear.' She picks up a pen and draws two lines on a piece of paper. 'It's on a graph, yes?'

I nod.

She continues, 'This line is the time that passes and this line is the experience of grief. Okay?'

I nod again, already feeling dismissive of what Nola is about to say because nothing that anyone else has ever said before has made any sense. Nola draws an x on the graph.

'This is the death—it indicates the beginning of our graph. And now this,' and she proceeds to draw haphazard, squiggly lines all over the graph, 'this is grief.'

It's a ridiculous unplanned mess of purple ink, and she says: 'There is no typical path, Ava. It is what it is and you feel what you feel. And it's crap. And it's going to keep being crap. Until one day it'll be a little less crap and I can't tell you when that will be, but I can tell you it will come. You've just got to wait it out.'

I feel the most overwhelming sense of relief. 'Thank you,' I say.

'Thank you?' She seems surprised. 'Most people feel extremely disappointed when I tell them this.'

'Nope, I just feel like that makes the most sense ever. The fact that you even acknowledged that it's shit. That helps.'

'I've never had anyone I love lose their battle with depression,' she says, 'but my dad died four years ago and I miss him every single day. I still catch myself instinctively picking up my phone to call him and then I realise I can't and it's—'

'So fucked,' I cut her off. 'I do that all the time and it's the stupid shit I want to tell her the most or text her when a song we like comes on or when I see something that I know she'd laugh at.' I pause. 'I feel like I will never be the same again.'

'You won't. You can't be. We're not fixed things, Ava. We change every single day. I mean there's things in our bodies that grow and die every single second. We're physically changing right now.' She stops and looks at me and I'm listening. Intently. 'You're not the same as you were before Kelly died. You are different. And part of your grief is grieving for who you were then, because some parts of that girl are gone.'

I don't know how to take this in, or what to say. It feels massive.

'But you're not dead, Ava. You're still here. So, we've got to start processing what this new Ava wants and how she wants to feel.'

'Yeah.' I take a big deep breath in. 'But it's hard.'

She smiles a big cheeky smile. 'Nah, not hard. It's so transient anyway, because we're always changing. Just take it, like, a week at a time and let future Ava worry about the other changes. Unless there's changes you know you want to make right now, then we can talk about them if you want.'

I do want. I so desperately want. I want to talk to her about the biggest change in my life right now: Gideon, or more specifically me and Gideon. I tell her all about my friend, about kissing him, about not being able to not kiss him when we're around each other anymore and I tell her about the fight, about what we said to each other.

'If you want to be my friend, Gideon, then stop trying to be my boyfriend,' I snapped at him when he tried to hold my hand as we walked down the street.

'I didn't mean—' He quickly pulled his hand away.

'You can't hold my hand in public, or buy me flowers, or write me poems or be so lovely all the time.'

I don't know why I said this, I liked it when he held my hand. But it felt so definite, it meant that he was sure about us, about what we were doing, and I wasn't sure at all.

He didn't say anything.

'Gideon?' I wanted to make sure he'd heard.

He did, because he just mumbled, 'I don't know what you want, Ava.'

Good point. I don't know what I want either. I knew I didn't want to hurt Gideon's feelings, but the look on his face showed me that that was exactly what I'd done.

'I think I should go,' I told him as he looked at me through his long eyelashes.

'Is that what you want?' he asked and again I said nothing.

Finally he said, 'If you want to be *my* friend, Ava, then you need to stop—' I wasn't sure if he'd finished the sentence or if there was more.

'What?' I asked.

'Leading me on. If you want to be my friend, Ava, then you need to stop leading me on.' His eyes quickly darted to mine and then to the floor, and the blood rushed from my head as I quickly tried to work out what to say.

Nola looks at me. 'Do you know what you want?'

'I know I don't want to hurt him.'

'Yeah, but what do you *want?*' Nola asks again.

'Him,' I say after a long pause and she nods.

I want him. All of him. All of it with him. I do, and that's petrifying.

GIDEON

There was a short note from Ava when I got home. It asked one question and had two tick boxes for my reply.

Go on a date with me?

Yes ☐   No ☐

The last time Ava and I talked I accused her of leading me on, so I was kind of surprised by this turn of events. Ava Spirini wants to go on a date with me. I've never been on a date before and my brain is immediately flooded with an onslaught of romantic possibilities and also possible disasters.

At work that night I hand her the card with the *yes* box ticked. She looks at it and smiles.

'Good.' She pauses, her eyebrows kind of dancing like she has a secret. 'Tomorrow? I'll pick you up at seven.'

Before she arrives I'm in a good place. Well, for me. I've only contemplated about three actual scenarios where I could ruin it. So, I've pre-prepared a range of varied and interesting conversation topics and I'm wearing my lucky jocks. I don't know what makes them lucky. They're just my *favourite*. But I figure I can use all the help I can get.

Ava knocks on the door at 7:04 p.m.—I know, because I'm waiting upstairs staring at the LCD screen of my clock. I walk down the stairs attempting to look cool but end up misjudging the bottom step and kind of tumble down in a thud to the floor. Ava and Susan both crack up laughing.

'Smooth, kiddo,' Susan whispers into my ear and I give her a sideways glance that she interprets correctly as 'HOLY SHIT I'M GOING ON A DATE AND I DON'T WANT TO FUCK IT UP AND PLEASE TELL ME THAT I'M NOT GOING TO FUCK IT UP AND EVERYTHING WILL BE AWESOME.'

She just smiles knowingly.

Ava and I walk in silence for a while; it's so weird that you can literally put your tongue inside someone else's mouth and then have nothing to talk about.

Then she says, 'I forgot to give you this,' and pulls out a small black plaited piece of leather with a tiny white flower stitched onto it. 'I made it. For you. Instead of flowers.' She's awkward as she ties it around my wrist, kind of giggling.

'Thank you.' I smile, looking at the wristband and then at her.

We walk a few more steps together and Ava holds my hand. Just slips her hand into mine and starts talking about something, except I'm not paying attention because I'm too focused on the way it feels for our palms to be touching.

Ava Spirini is holding my hand. In full view of the public so that anyone who happened to look at us walking together right now would assume that we were a couple. I wonder if they'd be right in assuming that. I hope so. Ava's hand in mine feels right.

Ava's grand date plan is for us to go trampolining. This is not something I would have expected, but it works out well, mostly. We bounce on trampolines and into foam pits, chase each other like idiots and run into trampoline walls. She laughs at how physically incompetent I am every time I fall over, trip or face-plant the tough bouncy mats, which is a lot. I get shown up by a group of eight-year-olds who challenge us to a slam-dunk competition. They all manage some kind of elaborate move to get the tiny foam ball into the hoop. I just end up doing the splits and pulling a muscle in my groin.

Ava holds out her hand to help me up. 'Come on, Skinny, before you disgrace your family any more.'

I hobble behind her, trying to convince her that I was robbed. She doesn't go for it. I do, however, beat Ava four times in a row on some shooting arcade game and feel like my masculinity is restored. We laugh and cheat on the games where you can win tokens. We win enough for us both to get pencil sharpeners with smiley faces on them.

'I have an idea,' Ava says. She grabs my wrist and threads my smiley face sharpener onto my wrist band. She does the same to the one she's wearing and then we have matching jewellery.

'Now we'll always have a reminder to be happy,' I grin, and she blushes a little. 'Or something else that isn't completely lame.'

She laughs.

She won't let me pay for anything the whole night and says it is her 'constitutional right as the inviter to make the invitee feel special'. I don't argue.

I think about how amazing I feel. I like that she's making an effort. I like that she wants to make me feel special. I like that she's thought about me when she wasn't with me.

AVA

I feel full with ice-cream and laughter and good conversation. When Gideon and I finally come up for air we've covered everything from our greatest fears to places we want to visit in the world to our favourite ninja turtle. He's told me all about his confusion about finishing school and his grand plans to write novels, and I tell him more stories about Kelly and how one day I'd like to go to Antarctica. I love how easy it is to talk to him. I told him things tonight that I haven't told anyone. Not even Kelly.

There's a few disgruntled teenagers in neon green T-shirts packing up chairs loudly around us, trying to make us leave; we just keep talking and giggling.

'Come on, I'll walk you home,' I tell him.

*

When we get to the door, we make stupid small talk about the stars and I wait for a lull in the conversation so I can kiss him. Finally he stops rambling and I go for it, I kiss him like my whole life depends on it.

He pulls away, smiling wide. 'Do you want to come in?'

'What about your parents?'

'They're out for the night, at a party, they're crashing there,' he says, and my stomach spasms with a mix of joy and nerves and I nod quickly and eagerly. I've never wanted anything, anyone, more.

GIDEON

I'm freaking out and all I can hear is my mums in my head, who are actually the last people you want to be thinking about when you have a girl in your room, sitting next to you on your bed, smiling at you.

In Grade 5 I was on the bus and Amanda Pearson asked me if I'd like to go out with her best friend, Emily Drake. I said yes. Emily Drake was pretty. I had no idea what you were meant to do when you went out with a girl. I wasn't allowed to go anywhere without my parents, so I told my mums about me going out with Emily and this is what they said: 'Girls are nervous too. Probably even more nervous than you, and we're going to guess that she's really, really hoping that the next time you see her you'll hold her hand. So even though you're nervous you're just going to have to be brave.'

Even though you're nervous you're just going to

have to be brave. Thanks, Mums.

I look at Ava and I do the first brave thing that comes to mind. I stand up and walk across the room. I stand up and walk across the room *away* from the amazing girl in my room. I stand up and walk across the room away from the amazing girl sitting on my bed. I stand up and walk across the room away from the amazing girl sitting on my bed, smiling at me. I take three strides across the room and I turn off the light.

'Gideon, what are you doing?' she asks.

I have no idea.

AVA

I smile so big that my face squishes and closes my eyes.
He's so cute and nervous. And I'm nervous. I've never
been this nervous. I've kissed loads of guys, including
Gideon. But now, this feels different. It feels huge. We
were doing fine, sitting close enough on the bed to be
near each other but leaving just enough space to not
actually touch.

Once we came upstairs we talked and smiled at each
other and I waited for him to kiss me this time, only
he hasn't yet. So then it got awkward and I started to
think that maybe he thought that this whole thing was
a really bad idea. And, because it's Gideon, it means he
doesn't know how to actually tell me that he invited me
up to his room to tell me that he doesn't like me like
that, that he was wrong and that he's realised he just
wants to be friends.

While I'm busy mulling all of this over in my head he gets up and turns off the light. It's now pitch black.

'Gideon, what are you doing?'

'Being brave.'

'What? Are you scared of the dark?'

'No.' He pauses. 'Of you.'

'You're scared of me?'

'Yup.'

So I stand up. The room is dark and I can barely see him at all; come on, eyes, hurry up and adjust, but it's taking too long, so I reach into my pocket and get my phone.

'Stay where you are,' I say.

GIDEON

The torch on her phone flicks on, pointing at the ground. I can just make out her silhouette as the light moves with each step. I'm pretty sure she's saying something, humming something, but my heart is beating in my ears and I can't really hear anything. So much for being brave.

Ava is right in front of me. She rests the phone on the bed, then one of her hands grabs my wrist as the other hand pads its way up my arm to my shoulder and my neck. She gently places two hands on my face.

'Gideon,' she whispers.

'Yeah?'

'You should kiss me now.' She stops for a second. 'If you want.'

Oh, how I want.

So I do. And she does. We don't stop for what feels

like my entire life up until this point and I don't want to ever stop. I kind of just want to melt into her, into the floor, into this moment and have it never end. It is exactly like it has been in my head the billion times I've played it out and also nothing like it at all.

And as it turns out, I don't need to be brave, because it all just kind of happens, like if you turn your brain off for just a second your body actually knows what to do. My hands are on her hips, under her shirt, touching the skin on her back, which is soft, so soft that I stop touching her and just look at her face. She looks kind of shy. Ava is never shy, so that makes me smile too.

'What?' she says.

'Just—' is all I can manage and she laughs and we stop and my heart is beating and I can feel her heart beating and my hands are shaking and our breath synchs up.

In.

Out.

In.

Out.

Ava hugs me. Squeezes me even, and I squeeze her back. Tight and desperate, like if I let her go she'll disappear and this moment will be over. She pulls back just enough to run one hand through my hair and onto my cheek and she kisses me again. It's urgent and fast and our tongues dart around each other's mouths and I'm clinging to her. One hand on her lower back, one hand on her neck, pressing her into me as close as I can, and she moves her hands over my cheeks, my shoulders my chest, she moves her hips into me and when we next break for air I'm positive my skin is actually tingling. Like fruit tingles when they first hit your tongue, but better. A billion times better.

I peel her top off over her head and we step and kiss and shuffle our way in the direction of the bed except we stumble and trip on something, trip over each other and we fall. This, I think, is fitting because I have. Fallen. For Ava. I'm sure of it.

I land on the floor with her on top of me and she laughs with her whole body; it shakes against mine as she laughs, her eyes crinkling shut as she lands her head on my chest and exhales a loud sigh. And it smacks me for a moment that this is the first time that I've heard her laugh like this. Seen it. Felt it. Like she can't help it. Like something has cracked and is pouring out, and it's catching because I can't help but laugh too. Laugh till tears well in my eyes and I can't get my breath. Then it smacks me that I've not heard myself, felt myself, laugh like this in the longest time either.

'I can't remember the last time I felt this —' Ava stops herself, but I know exactly what she's going to say.

I know exactly what she means, too. Except I've *never* been this happy. Ever.

AVA

I pull my mouth away from his but stay close to his face. 'Do you want to?'

He kisses me. Nods. Pulls back his mouth but remains close enough to reply.

'Yes.'

Good.

I pull his shirt up over his head and kiss his neck. As I'm kissing his skin I remind myself that this is his first time. That when he talks about losing his virginity this will be the moment he will talk about. I'm the girl he'll remember, and so I make a quick promise to myself that, yes, I will make it happen. And, yes, I will do everything in my power to make sure that this becomes a memory he'll be stoked to talk about.

GIDEON

I AM HAVING SEX. I'M ACTUALLY HAVING SEX.

It is exactly like I thought it would be and nothing like I thought it would be all at the same time. It feels so fucking amazing. My eyes are shut tight and I'm so aware of my breath, shallow but deep at the same time. I can feel Ava's hands on my chest as she manoeuvres up and down and I'm just in. I am in it. In the moment and a girl and OH MY FREAKING GOODNESS. It's so obvious to me now why people lose their shit about sex because it's quite possibly the best thing ever invented.

Ava leans into my neck and murmurs, 'We need a condom.'

OH SHIT A CONDOM. YES. I immediately tense as a wave of disappointment washes over me. I don't have any condoms.

'I don't have any,' I whisper.

'What?' She stops moving but we stay connected.

'I'm on the pill. But,' she replies.

'But?'

She exhales disappointment. 'We better. We better not. You know.'

'Yes. Sure. Yes. Of course.'

She kisses me again and we move together but I push her away. 'Okay, okay, we need to stop.'

Ava smiles and manoeuvres her body until she's lying next to me.

'I'm so sorry,' she whispers in my ear.

'What? Why?'

'That's so disappointing,' and she starts to laugh, and I start to laugh and we can't stop laughing until we start kissing again and Ava's hand moves down my body, past my belly button, and everything feels incredible and then I can't think at all, because OH MY GOD YES.

AVA

I sit in the shower. The hot water powering over me. I cross my legs and close my eyes and take deep breaths. If I get calm enough I can conjure her in my head, imagine what would happen if she was still alive.

She's lying across my bed, her pink bandana tied in a knot on her forehead, and she's smiling at me as I kneel on the floor and squeal into the bed, giddy.

'Tell me!' she screams, laughing.

'It's embarrassing.'

'It's not embarrassing. Did you do it?'

'No.'

'Why not?'

'Because he's a—'

'I forget he's a virgin.' She pauses. 'So what did you do?'

I look her in the eye and smile, I feel my face flush.

She jumps to her knees and grabs my face with both hands. 'Did you have a—?' she asks, madly searching my face and smiling wide. I nod and my smile cracks and she squeals, 'Shut *up*. Really? Tell me everything.'

'Oh my god. It was so good, Kels.'

'This is the best!' she screams, lying quickly back and kicking her legs in the air and laughing.

'How?' she asks.

'He did it, with, you know,' I hold my hand up and wiggle it in the air. I'm so embarrassed and happy and find all of this so hilarious but if I didn't share this with her I feel like I might just have burst.

'Really? Who'd have thought that white boy had moves.' She's taking the piss, laughing. 'This is so good. So. So good.' She laughs as I lie next to her and hold a pillow tight to my chest.

'Have you ever before?' I ask and I can't believe that Kelly and I have never talked about orgasms, or that we have in a larger metaphorical *Cosmo*-type way but not about each other specifically.

'Not with someone else. On my own, yeah. Heaps,' she mumbles.

'I hadn't,' I tell her, and wait.

'Not ever?' She spins, looking at me as I shake my head and hide my face under the cushion.

'WHAT?' she screams. 'Ava! That's terrible.' She whacks me again with the cushion. 'And now that just makes this even more awesome.' She lies next to me. 'You really like him, don't you?'

I nod. Yeah.

*

Then she's gone and I'm in the shower and the water is cold and I feel giddy and sad all at the same time. God. I miss her. For the past two days these flashes of things with Gideon will sweep into my brain and make me feel nervous and flushed. Like when I'm washing up, or at TAPs or brushing my teeth and then *wham* some kind of memory from the last few times we've hung out will take over my brain and make me blush. In the past these moments would make me feel embarrassed, but not now, I just feel a burst of excitement. It's weird knowing that we're the only two people in the world who know what's happened between us.

And I can't help it, I just end up thinking about everyone else having sex. Not picturing them or anything. Just thinking that there are all these people in the world who know these completely secret things about each other, and they're the only two people in the world who know them. I just think it's fascinating.

I've had sex before. With three people. I've kissed thirteen boys and two girls. There's something different about making out with Gideon, though: I don't think. All the other times you kind of have those moments where you stop thinking, but they're just fleeting, you know? Some thought will eventually wander in, about how you look or the light or about weird things the other person does or just feeling desperately fat and dumb. I always feel so nervous. Not that I'd ever say that to any of the others. I guess because I spend most of the time in my head. Another memory collides with the present and my smile is so big it forces my eyes shut as I think about our conversation.

'How did you know how to do that?' I asked him, sweaty and a little embarrassed, but totally relaxed.

'I googled it,' Gideon says under his breath.

'*What?* You googled it? What did you google?'

'That's between me and Google.'

'So your internet ban is lifted?'

'No. But I thought this was a particularly important exception.' He is shirtless, lying on his side next to me. I'm lying on my back and I glance up at him. There's a silence. Gideon smiles at me; his eyes don't move from mine. He looks so different, so chilled. It's weird.

'You look so proud of yourself.' I cover my eyes with my hands, feeling oddly shy.

'I am *so* proud of myself,' he laughs.

After the condom incident we haven't attempted it again; it's like we're both too nervous to bring it up. Which I don't understand, seeing as other parts of our bodies have touched private parts of each other's bodies, but for some reason talking about condoms suddenly seems too huge or like actually admitting the fact that we're going to have sex. It's not like you make out and then talk about making out.

It feels like we're sitting on the edge of an aeroplane that's thousands of feet in the air and we're about to jump out of the plane but we're both waiting for the other person to jump first. Someone has got to do something.

•

'I don't know why you need me here,' Minda asks. We're at Coles, in the aisle with the condoms.

'I've never bought them before,' I mutter, pretending I'm staring at the men's razors while trying to sideways-glance at the different packets. Minda marches straight up to them and starts quite loudly reading out the descriptions on the packets. 'Thin, regular, flavoured, large.' She looks at me. 'Does he have a large penis?'

I am mortified. I feel my cheeks flush bright red as I look at her and my eyebrows plead with her to stop.

She just smiles wide. 'Feather-lite, ribbed...oooh, glow in the dark?' She picks up the box and starts reading. 'These freak me out. Why do you need them to glow in the dark?' She shakes her head and I continue to stare at the men's hair-growth shampoo with such intensity that the image may very well burn my retinas. Minda picks up a box and passes it to me. 'Buy these.'

So I do and am grateful when the whole ordeal is over.

'Who is this guy?' Minda asks as we eat fries in the food court.

'We work together.' I smile. I don't want to be one of those girls who lose their brain over a guy. 'He's thoughtful and lovely and sweet and funny. He cracks me up,' I say, leaning my head in my hands and looking at Minda.

'You've had sex before, yeah?' she asks, and I nod. 'Then why are you so nervous?'

I think about it. 'He's the first guy that I've actually really, really liked. It feels different.'

'It is different.' Minda's green hair flicks across her face as she quickly responds.

'It is?'

'Don't get me wrong—the mechanics are exactly the same,' she says, 'and it can be pretty good when you don't like them. But when you do and it's good, then it's *really* good.' Minda smiles to herself, and I bite on the end of my straw.

'Just do it, already.' She throws a chip at my face and I look at her, pretending to be pissed off.

Fine. I think I just will then.

•

I put the record on and turn to look at him sitting on the edge of the bed, jotting words into a notebook. Biting his lip, his eyebrows furrowed together as his hand loops around the page trying to catch whatever thought he's had. His brown curls sit loosely on his forehead, kind of bouncing with the movement of his hand. He makes my insides feel like they're all squished together and pulsating some kind of liquid joy through my body. I wonder if this is what it feels like when you're in love. I stride over and take the book and pen out of his hand.

'Oh, hello,' he murmurs as I straddle him and grab his face to kiss him. His hands are on my lower back.

The kiss is slow and sweet but within seconds it quickens, it's like we can't get close enough and I can feel his hands move under my shirt and touch the skin at my waist. I kiss his neck and run my hands down his sides and back up over the front of his chest until I get to the top button of his shirt. I undo it. I undo all of them, one by one, but we don't stop kissing. We are so close together and we're both breathing fast. I pull his shirt open and he shimmies it off and throws it on the floor. I go to kiss him but he stops and just looks me straight in the eye. I'm kind of amazed by how good it is.

His hands trace the line of my jaw to my chin, down my neck and onto my chest and he stops at my first button. Still looking at me, smiling. His breath is hard in his chest as he undoes each of my buttons slowly. Running his fingers in a line and kissing each spot as he goes. He slips my shirt off and it drops to the floor and we fall back onto the bed rolling over so Gideon lies on top of me. I rub my fingers up and down his back, tracing the line of his waistband.

He undoes his shorts and tries to fling them off but the angle is weird. I start to giggle and he laughs, frustrated, as he shifts his body and pushes them all the way down and kicks them off. He is naked, we laugh as I straddle him again, kissing his neck and his chest. Unhook my bra and fling it onto the floor. Gideon shakes his head, kind of stunned.

Then his hands glide up my hips over my boobs and across my shoulders to the back of my neck, where he pulls me into him and we kiss, then I undo my skirt and we pull it over my head, laughing when the button gets stuck in my hair and Gideon has to help me untangle it.

I kiss his chest and his nipples, and his head rolls back as he breathes out loudly. I kiss across his shoulder and the line of his arm muscle. I kiss his forearm. He tenses a little so I look at him as I run my lips over the skin—all the little scars—and he lets me do it for a moment before pulling me back towards him as we kiss quick and urgent and push our bodies into each other. It's the hottest thing ever. How much I want him.

GIDEON

I HAVE HAD SEX. I HAVE ACTUALLY HAD SEX.
FULL AND COMPLETE AND FINISHED SEX.
WITH A CONDOM. I HAVE HAD SEX WITH A
CONDOM.

I don't really feel different, though. I thought I might.
But I don't. I feel like when someone tells you to watch
a really good TV show and it ends and you are deeply
satisfied but also a little disappointed because now it's
over and the mystery and anticipation of watching the
awesome TV show is now over. It won't feel that way
ever again. Even if you watch it all over again it won't
be the same. It's how I feel now.

Although that feeling is being quickly replaced by a
whole swirl of other more important thoughts, such as:

1. I've never realised how small our shower is; I'm realising this now because Ava and I are both in our shower.

2. Shower heads are not made to wet two people at the same time.

3. Ava is hilarious. She has washed her wild hair and stuck it up like a troll doll and asked me if I liked her new hairstyle. Of course I do. I like everything about her.

It turns out that Ava and I both had condom-buying adventures and I laugh as she tells me about her experience in the Coles aisle. Mine was similar, except I did a very, very purposeful tactical trip up the aisle as reconnaissance to ensure I knew the exact location of the condoms. I then waited by the milk until it became relatively empty and marched back up the aisle with one hand outstretched to grab the first box I could. I did not slow down as I walked straight up to the self-checkout. I was in and out of the place in four minutes and twenty-seven seconds total. I timed it.

Ava and I are kissing and I get soap in my eyes, and it becomes a thing as I try and get it out. Then there's a double-tap knock on the door.

'Gids, we're home,' my mum yells.

'Shit,' Ava mouths.

I shriek, 'Okay,' and we stare at each other, wide-eyed. All of a sudden I'm desperately aware of how naked I am. I turn off the shower and grab a towel and throw one to Ava.

'*What do we do?*' she whispers, giggling nervously.

'*I don't know,*' I whisper back. I can't think straight.

I wrap the towel around my waist and signal for Ava to stay put. Ever so gently I open the door and walk out of the bathroom and shut the door behind me and take two steps into the hallway. Susan comes out of their bedroom with a washing basket.

'Hey kiddo.'

'Hey!' My voice comes out way too loud.

'How was your day?'

'*Good.* Yeah, good.' But my brain is flashing up these quick images from this afternoon that make my stomach tense and my whole body blush.

'School good?'

'Good. Yeah,' I sound like a cave man. Me Gideon. Naked girl in shower. Mum. Embarrassing.

'This is your stuff,' she says, walking towards me.

'I'll take it.' Damn—too enthusiastic. 'I can do it. Yeah. I'll put it away.' Now I appear to be mimicking a robot.

'Okay.' She hands me the basket, looking amused. 'What do you want for dinner?'

'I don't. I dunno,' I mumble as she turns and starts walking back up the hallway and I am very, very aware that there is a very naked girl in our bathroom.

'I've got to do some work so I'll just be in my room,' I say.

'Okay.'

She walks down the stairs, completely oblivious to the fact that her only son is no longer a virgin. That he's had sex. In her house. Within the last hour.

I wait till I can hear them in the kitchen then I go back to the bathroom. I open the door and Ava stands there with the towel wrapped around her body, her hair swept back off her face, saturated, wide-eyed, but smiling. She starts to laugh. So I start to laugh. I put my finger to my mouth as I grab her hand and pull her towards me. I kiss her and wrap my arm around her waist, pushing her in front of me but still holding on to her as we tiptoe together back up the hallway towards my room. My heart is racing.

'Gids, how's Chinese?' Susan's head appears at the bottom of the stairs. She has a clear view of Ava and me. We both freeze. I slowly turn and look at her, my jaw clenched tight as I wait for her reaction.

'Oh.' A small sound of shock. 'Oh.' More purposeful.

'What?' Mum appears behind her, because this situation clearly isn't awkward enough. 'Oh.' Then: 'Hello, Ava.' She says each word slowly.

'Hello,' Ava smiles and grabs my hand.

Kill. Me. Now.

•

'So, we just need to talk about it,' Mum says, ripping the bandaid off the tension that has seethed ever since they caught me and Ava naked in the hallway. Ava went home—she got dressed, apologised profusely and bolted all in about 12.5 seconds—while I waited in my room pondering if I actually needed to see my parents ever again.

When finally Susan yelled *Dinner* I went down and we all ate in silence in front of the TV.

But once the plates are cleared Mum flicks off the TV and announces that the conversation I've so been dreading is in fact about to take place.

'Do we, though?' I put my head in my hands and lean my elbows on my knees.

'Yes. Yup. Um-mmm, yes we do,' Mum gabbles.

'This doesn't need to be awkward.' Susan grins and rests her hand on the fireplace. Mum and I both stare at her like she's deranged. 'We just need to talk about some boundaries and about safety,' she adds, smiling even wider.

She is loving this. Susan, like Annie, is not backward in coming forward. She sits very comfortably in awkward places and nothing fazes her at all. Whereas Mum and I have the same flight response when anything is uncomfortable, and recoil like an AK-47 at the slightest whiff of conflict.

Susan doesn't lie. Ever. So, any time you ask her a question you have to be prepared to get an honest answer. Like the time I was in Grade 4 and Annie was in Grade 6. Annie asked her what a dildo was. I was not prepared for her answer. I will never be prepared for her answers. Whereas with Mum you get a more floral approach, lots of metaphors and blushing. When I was sick their contrasting approaches worked at different times. Mum telling me I would be okay and it was a battle we could fight and win; Susan telling me to take my tablets or else and that she was hiding all of the sharp things in the house in case I wanted to cut myself.

Susan starts. 'We need to talk about the responsibility that comes with sex. Consent. Protection. Pregnancy—'

'Diseases,' Mum adds.

'Oh god,' I murmur.

'And this right here, mate—if you can't talk about it then you shouldn't be doing it. You and Ava have got to talk about this stuff,' Susan says, gesticulating madly.

'Okay. We are. Do. We will.' I don't know what I'm saying. I'm just trying to stop it before it gets any worse.

'Good. Okay. It's okay.' Mum is red like a beetroot. 'Sex is like a flower.'

'*What?*' Susan says, laughing.

'I'm just—oh god,' Mum mutters.

'Thing is,' Susan goes on, 'I don't know how I feel about you having sex in the house.'

'Suse,' Mum says under her breath.

'What? I don't. But then I don't want you to go and do it somewhere else. Do you have condoms?'

'Yes,' I squeak.

'Gideon!' Mum squeals.

'What?'

'That means you're actually doing—' Mum stops herself and Susan chimes in.

'Okay. Good. That's good. You made good choices.'

Mum pats my leg and stares wide-eyed at Susan. When will this end?

'Do you actually have condoms?' Susan says.

I quickly interject, 'Yes, I bought them.' The last thing I need is a trip to Woolies with my mothers to buy condoms. I can just picture the argument in the aisle about which brand is best for durability and ethical production...Besides, what would either of them know about buying condoms?

'Okay,' Mum exhales.

'Okay.' Susan nods.

'Okay,' I sit back in my chair, relaxing a little. Surely this is done now?

'I think we should talk about the vagina,' Susan smiles enthusiastically.

'*Suse!*' Mum cuts her off.

'Is it like a flower?' I ask, and Susan cracks up while daggers shoot from Mum's eyes.

'It's nothing like a flower, mate,' Susan says, and I laugh.

'More like a box of cereal?' I smirk.

'Like a Tahitian waterfall,' Susan says.

'Great, now you're both taking the piss out of me. Excellent.'

'Sorry Mum.'

'Just. Be a...Be kind. Girls are nervous too. Just make sure she's...' Mum trails off, unsure what to say.

Susan cuts in: 'Make sure you're both having fun.'

'Okay. Are we done now?'

'Yes.'

'Thank god.'

They tell me they love me and I feel all levels of embarrassed, giddy and weird. I then think about how weird that must've been for them and I feel grateful that it was over quickly and that they didn't say anything too dumb. I take a moment to predict how long it will take for them to tell Annie and when she will call; I predict ten hours.

Two days. It takes two days for Annie to call. She was on the back end of a trip in Marrakech and didn't get Susan's message until she landed; then she called straight away. She gives me a heap of shit and makes me high-five her hand on the screen.

'This is the most brilliant thing ever.'

'Me losing my virginity?'

'No. You being sprung. I can't believe I'm not there. Mum will not be coping.'

'She's not, and Susan is thriving. We were watching a movie last night and she pointed at the actress and asked if I would, and I quote, "go her".'

Annie loses her shit and starts laughing uncontrollably, loud and open-mouthed.

'What did you say?'

'I said sure, and guess what she said?' I can feel my face blushing even now as Annie waits, wide-eyed. 'She said, "That's my boy, I would too." She is using all of this as an excuse to make everything about sex. She's obsessed.'

Annie is crying and panting with laughter. I tell her about the weird sex-ed chat and eventually I tell her about Ava, she asks questions and I answer and she seems genuinely happy for me. I'm genuinely happy for me.

AVA

The last few weeks have become a blur of lovely moments and kissing. I decide to do what Gideon would do and write a list of my top five so I can remember them.

1. MUSIC AND BED

I feel like so much of the time that Gideon and I spend together, the times that I love the most, are when we are just hanging out, lying on either of our beds, listening to music and talking. Not even talking about anything too deep. Being together, making each other laugh and making out. The more comfortable Gideon feels around me the more interesting I find him. He's so smart and knows stuff about the world and politics and he has opinions about world issues that I know nothing about. Music is so important to him, or lyrics, mostly. We'll spend whole nights with him playing me his favourite tracks, pointing out his most favourite lines. I love his brain.

2. WALLFLOWERS AND BRIDESMAIDS

Gideon made me watch *Perks of Being a Wallflower,* it's his favourite book.

'Is this where you got the idea to write me a letter from?' I asked and he nodded. I'm so glad he did. We ate an entire roll of pre-made cookie dough and sobbed through the end. It felt weird to cry about something that was external from me, but I saw so much of Gideon in the movie.

I, however, made him watch *Bridesmaids* because it's mine and Kelly's favourite movie. If that right there doesn't highlight the stark contrast between Gideon and me then I don't know what will. He laughed, a lot. But he laughed in different bits to me and Kel. It was weird. But I like that I can talk to him about her.

3. BOYFRIEND

Gideon is a hand-holder. If my hand is near him he will hold it. I like that about him. We have been spending all of our free time together, holding hands. We both go to school and then end up at each other's houses in the afternoon. If we're rostered on at different times at Magic Kebab the other comes and hangs out. We spend all our weekends together.

It was natural to assume that this was an actual thing between us, but we hadn't talked about it. One afternoon we were at my house and my Yiayia called.

I put her on speaker so Gideon could hear her talk. Her accent is really thick and she gets words wrong and I find her really funny. We were just chatting and Gideon listened intently, raising his eyebrows when she said amusing and racist things and laughing at her quietly as she waffled on about her day, my Pappou, my cousins, things she'd cooked and when Dad and I were coming to visit. She asked me what I was doing and out of my mouth fell the words, 'Yiayia, I'm just hanging out with my boyfriend.' Gideon stared at me. And my mouth flew open. *Boyfriend*, he mouthed laughing.

'Oh, a boyfriend, Ava, you too young to have a boyfriend,' Yiayia sneered.

'No, Yiayia, he's nice, you'll like him.' I could feel my cheeks blush and Gideon grabbed my hand and held it.

'Is he a good boy?'

'Yes.'

'Is he smart?'

'Yes. He's a writer, Yiayia.' He kissed my hand and I shook my head. So embarrassed.

'Ohh. Is he white?'

'Yiayia!' I yelled, shaking my head at her, and Gideon cracked up laughing. *See?* I mouthed to Gideon. *She's so inappropriate.*

'What? I like to know about this boyfriend. You send me a picture on the mobile.'

'Okay. Love you.' And after she'd sung me the chorus to *You Are My Sunshine* she hung up.

'Your boyfriend, huh?' Gideon smiled, smug.

'Well, aren't you?'

'I don't know. Am I?'

I rolled my eyes at him. 'Yes,' and the biggest smile swept across his cheeks.

'Will you be my girlfriend, Ava?'

I shrugged and he grabbed my shoulders in his hands, getting close to my face. 'Yes. I suppose.' I smiled as he kissed me.

4. ICE-SKATING

We decided to go ice-skating because Gideon had never been and I thought it would be fun. I was wrong. Neither of us could really get the hang of it and we'd either cling to the edge or each other, which was a terrible idea, because we'd just end up making each other fall down. We spent most of the time lying on the ice, entangled, laughing at the other trying to get up. Gideon's legs are so long that he looked like a baby giraffe trying to stand for the first time.

At one point on the ice, Gideon looked at me and said, 'When we were little Annie told me this story about a kid who went ice-skating and fell over and some other kid skated over his fingers and chopped them all clean off.' He then re-enacted how he'd skated for the rest of that trip with his hands tucked in to his body up against his chest. We both tried to stand up like this and a Year 8 kid who worked at the rink had to skate over and tell us to leave. We were bruised, wet, shivering and laughing hysterically. It was the best, worst date ever.

5. THE FORMAL

I will never forget how Gideon asked me to the
formal. He'd been acting weird all afternoon, and had
said we weren't allowed to go in his bedroom because
his parents had just had the carpets cleaned and they
were drying. He kept ducking off for long periods of
time. Eventually he came back, took my hands and
said: 'I have a surprise.'

We walked up to his room and he stood behind
me and covered my eyes with his hands as he pushed
me forward into the room.

There was some lovely song playing on the record
player and when he took his hands away from my
eyes he'd hung fairy lights from every surface of his
ceiling and walls so his room had turned into this
glittering paradise.

He nervously started to pace, grabbing a rose
from his desk and handing it to me. 'Am I meant
to get down on one knee?' he asked and my heart
stopped beating for a second before he shook his head
and started to ramble.

'I know it's an archaic gendered rite of passage
where people put all this pressure on one night
to be perfect, and they spend all this unnecessary
money, but I thought that maybe…if you wanted to
wear a nice dress…or maybe not a dress, that was
presumptuous of me, you can wear whatever you
want. We could. If you wanted to. You can say no
because I wasn't even going to go anyway and you
and I could just hang out and do something else.' He

stopped himself and I laughed at him. 'Ava, do you want to go to the formal with me?'

'Nah,' I said.

'Oh, good. I'm glad that's cleared up.'

Then I touched his face with my hand.

'Of course I'll go to the formal with you.'

GIDEON

'Do a spin,' Annie says in the screen, as I stand back and show her my suit. 'You look so handsome,' Annie squeals.

'Thanks,' I mutter.

'You look good, Gids.' Annie smiles knowingly. I feel good. Things are better than good. They're fucking golden. School is so close to being finished I can almost taste it. I have a girlfriend. I'm okay. Everything is okay. Except for one thing I've been thinking about a lot.

'There's one more thing,' I say. 'I've written her a poem.'

'You have? Read it to me.'

'No. It's embarrassing.'

'Please?' Annie puts her hands under her chin, smiling sweetly.

'Fine.' I protest but I was secretly hoping this would

be her response. I want to get her advice about whether I should give it to Ava at the formal. I reach over for my notebook.

'Don't laugh.'

'I most definitely will not laugh.'

I take a big breath, I'm already blushing, and start to read.

you make me write love poems when they've only ever been sad / I wish I could've pre-empted you / armed myself with a paper and a quill / cause I don't ever want to miss a moment with you / I want to write pages and pages / a whole PhD, cause my thesis would be clear / I just want to become a master of you, dear.

I can see nothing but the drape of your hair / the weight of your stare / electricity in your touch / you are so bright / your smile, too much / too much for this poet to comprehend / to find the right words / for you.

i've been reading poetry like its coming into fashion / trying to match words to this passion / sylvia wrote a mad girl's love song / shakespeare a glove upon that cheek / blake wrote about love in winds and how for her he'd seek / e.e wanted to carry your heart / but none of their art / compares to words I have / for you.

and it's exactly as they say / and not right at all / even the greatest poet couldn't describe the depths of this fall / for you.

I slowly look up at the screen and all I can see is Annie's watery eyes staring back at me as she murmurs this giddy 'nawww' sound.

'It's lame, isn't it?' I ask.

'Not even a little bit. It's beautiful, Gids.'

'Really? Do you think it'll freak her out?'

'I don't know. Do you?'

'Maybe a little. I don't know how she feels. I know she likes me. A lot. But, love. It feels pretty big to tell her. I don't know. I think it's too soon.'

'You'll know when, the moment will happen. Don't stress. She must really be something.'

'She is amazing.'

'Oh, little brother, I'm so happy for you. I'm also sad, because this means my plan of getting you over here is never going to work, is it?'

I shake my head.

'Damn it,' she mutters as the screen freezes and her face distorts. The messenger window pops up.

Internet is being weird.

You are amazing.

Be brave, little brother.

Love you.

Being brave would mean telling Ava how I feel. What have I got to lose? Apart from everything.

AVA

I swish the fabric in my giant skirt. 'You look beautiful,' my Dad smiles, taking photos on his phone, and I feel it. When Gideon sees me he blushes a little but doesn't say anything. I've actually made him speechless. I should straighten my hair and wear a push-up bra more often. His mums shake hands with my dad and we stand awkwardly as they take their photos and we smile.

It feels weird that you can know someone for such a short amount of time and then not be able to imagine your life without them. Gideon and I have fallen quickly into a pretty comfortable place that looks very much like what a happy couple looks like. And I feel happy—actually, really, happy—eighty per cent of the time. The other twenty per cent I just feel sad that all of this good stuff is happening and that Kelly's not here to share it with me.

I've been trying my best all day to push the melancholy away but it's like it's swirling around my insides making everything feel heavy. Kelly and I had spent hours talking about the formals we'd go to and what we'd wear and how fun they would be. She should be here and she's not. And even though I feel happy and beautiful and like I want to have an amazing time tonight, I really do, moments like this remind me that she's not coming back. She's gone.

It makes the cracks in my heart that feel like they've been repairing themselves break all over again.

GIDEON

Ava looks out-of-this-world beautiful, like stop-the-words-from-exiting-my-mouth, make-my-body-long-for-her beautiful. I had zero intention of ever attending my formal so it feels a bit crazy that in just a couple of months I've managed to do these normal things. Meet a girl, become friends with that girl, kiss that girl, have sex with that girl, for god's sake. Calling that girl my girlfriend and now going to my formal with that girl is just beyond ridiculous. Anything feels possible now. Not exactly because of Ava, but because all of these previously impossible things turned out to be entirely possible.

I can't stop staring at her across the back seat of the car. She holds my hands tight and I squeeze them to make sure this is all real, but something doesn't feel right. Ava hasn't said much all night.

'Are you okay?' I ask.

'Yeah.'

'Are you sure? You just seem a bit...quiet.'

'I'm just thinking,' she says and my heart sinks a little. What is she thinking about? Is it bad? Is it about me?

'What about?' I ask.

Ava looks out the window, and then slowly turns to face me. 'I just miss her.'

Of course it's not about you, you selfish dickhead. 'I know,' I say.

She tries to smile. 'I just wish she was here.' I can see the tears in her eyes start to well.

'Oh, Ava, it's okay. It'll be okay. We'll have a good time. We'll dance like idiots and you'll forget—'

'I don't want to forget,' she snaps. I've said the wrong thing. That's not what I meant. Fuck.

'No, I don't mean forget Kelly, I just mean, forget that...' I don't know what I'm trying to say. 'You'll forget that you're sad,' I mumble, but it hasn't worked, Ava has let go of my hands.

'Sometimes I'm just sad, Gideon. Sorry if I'm ruining your perfect night.'

'No. No. Ava. That's not what I meant. Shit.'

Is this our first fight? Is this a fight? *Fix it, Gideon. Fix it.*

Silence. Neither of us says anything for what feels like ages.

'I'm sorry,' she finally mumbles, patting my leg and looking at me. 'I just feel weird.'

'I know. It makes complete sense that you would feel that way. Of course you miss her tonight.' Ava softens a little and I feel a little relieved. 'We don't even have to go if you don't want,' I say.

'But you look so handsome,' she says, and I laugh.

Ava breathes in deep. 'No. We'll have a good time. We will. I'm fine.' She exhales loudly. 'Yup. Let's have a good time.' I can't work out if she's trying to convince me or herself.

But by the time we get to the hotel Ava and I are laughing and it's like the weirdness in the car is definitely behind us. We hit the dancefloor like it's what we were designed to do. We don't talk to anyone else. We're in our own bubble trying to make each other laugh the loudest with stupid dance moves or by madly singing along to the songs. I don't even care that I'm the world's shittest dancer; I look like a broken pogo stick with a curly wig balanced on the top.

But I don't care. All I care about is being here with her. She is all I care about. It's the worst feeling knowing that Ava is upset, but what's worse is knowing that there's absolutely nothing I can do to fix it.

AVA

I sit on the edge of my chair in the darkened room, trying to catch my breath, watching the dancefloor while I wait for Gideon to get back from the toilet. It is going off. Teachers are doing their daggiest moves, most of the girls have abandoned their heels and there's a group of boys laughing loudly. Lincoln is one of them. They synchronise their shoulders and shimmy back and forth. He looks happy. I laugh at them—right at the exact moment he exits the dancefloor. Our eyes lock. Lincoln nods at me and I grin. It's the first interaction we've had since Kelly's birthday.

He sent me one text a few days after, it was in the early hours of the morning and all it said was: *hey*. I ignored it.

I look back to where he's standing and he holds his phone in the air, staring at me. I don't know what he means. He points to his phone, so I grab my purse and pull my mobile out. There's a text from Lincoln.

Hi.

Hello. I text back without thinking.

My phone vibrates. *You look nice.*

Thank you. I hit send. And then start typing again. *So do you.*

I watch him read my message. He smiles then starts to type something, except he stops and looks away for a moment before he starts typing again. I watch my phone, waiting. Until finally...

Sorry.

That's it. I don't know what to say. Part of me wants to ask him what part he's sorry for exactly. Part of me is just glad he even said it. Part of me doesn't know what to think. My phone vibrates in my hand. *Want to dance?* I smile and look up at Lincoln and nod. I do.

Lincoln walks towards me, starting to dance. When I reach him he holds his hand out, I take it and he spins me around.

'You look very beautiful, Aves.' He slurs a little as he puts his arm around my waist and moves us from side to side.

'You're drunk.' I shake my head at him. 'But thank you.'

'It's my formal.' He smiles. We don't say anything, we just dance. 'So—' He laughs.

'So.' I look at his face, and my heart pangs because all I can see is Kelly. They have the same smile, the same eyes. She's not here and she should be. 'She would've loved this,' I say.

Lincoln stops dancing and I worry for a second that he's going to freak out, but he doesn't. 'Yeah. She would have.'

Lincoln pulls me closer so we're hugging, but our feet keep moving from side to side, so we're still technically dancing. It feels weird and safe and wrong and comfortable all at the same time. I know I should move away but I can't make my body actually back away from the embrace.

He whispers in my ear, 'I've missed you.'

I lean back slightly and look at his face, expecting him to immediately take it back, but he doesn't. He's being serious. I don't know what to say. But I don't have to say anything because he quickly spins me out and I go flying, the shock and the speed making me laugh, and that's when I see Gideon standing at the side of the dancefloor. Staring at us; looking pained.

My stomach twists and I let go of Lincoln as Gideon steps towards me.

'Who's this guy?' Lincoln jokes.

'This is Gideon,' I say, smiling, trying to keep the mood light. 'He's—' but Gideon cuts me off.

'Her boyfriend,' he spits, aggressive.

I watch as Lincoln's shoulders tense. 'Boyfriend?' Lincoln looks at me. I nod. He smiles, amused. Looks Gideon up and down. '*You're* her boyfriend?'

'Yeah, I am.' Gideon grabs my hand and pulls me towards him a little too intensely. He realises instantly that it was too hard and looks at me, apologising with his eyes, but he doesn't let go of my hand. I feel weird.

'Woah, mate, calm down. We're just dancing. Just two friends dancing.' Lincoln grabs my other hand and tries to move me around like he was before. I let go of both of them and step back.

Gideon moves towards Lincoln, closing in, and pokes him in the chest. 'I know all about you, Lincoln.'

What is happening? What is Gideon doing?

'What do you mean by that?' Lincoln pokes him back and then looks at me. 'What does he mean by that, Aves?'

'Gideon, calm down.' I grab his hand and pull on his shoulder, trying to get him away from Lincoln, but they're staring each other down. 'What are you doing?' I lean up and whisper in his ear.

'I'm sticking up for you,' he hisses back.

I reef him around to face me. 'I don't need you to stick up for me.'

'God! It's like you lose your fucking head around this jerk, Ava. Or don't you remember what he did?'

'Oi! Back off, dickhead. Ava can do what she likes,' Lincoln says.

'No, she can't,' Gideon spits.

'*Excuse* me?' I say, shocked.

'I didn't mean that. I just mean'—he looks at me, his eyes big, pleading. '*He* hit you.'

'Is that what you told him? Ava? That was an accident,' Lincoln scoffs.

'That's what I said.' I look at Lincoln, then back to Gideon. 'Calm. Down.'

'She doesn't need you anymore. She's got me.' Gideon looks directly at Lincoln.

'Oh really?' Lincoln bumps his chest into Gideon's but Gideon doesn't back off. *This can't be happening.*

'Both of you, stop!' They're chest to chest with their eyes locked, looking like they're going to murder each other. Gideon is shaking. I start to pull him away.

'She's a good root, isn't she, mate?' Lincoln snarls.

And everything falls away. I can't move. I can't hear anything, except this whooshing sound. My heart beats hard in my chest. Gideon is right in Lincoln's face saying something when Lincoln pushes him. Everything slows down as I watch Gideon stumble back and then immediately step forward with his fist outstretched as it pummels directly into Lincoln's face.

Gideon hits him. Punches him in the nose, hard. Lincoln falls back and lands on the floor with a thud.

Everything comes back into the moment and I can hear Lincoln groaning and Gideon panting and I step in between them. Lincoln is bleeding and Gideon is frozen, looking at his hand.

'Ava, I...' Gideon murmurs and Lincoln mutters something. Not really words, just this deep grunt. He jumps up. 'You fucking piece of shit.' Wiping his nose with the back of his hand, smearing blood across his cheek. He launches at Gideon so I push him backwards, trying everything I can to get him to look at me, to get him to focus on me and not on killing Gideon. I grab his face, one palm on each cheek—begging him to look at me but he won't, because he's too busy pushing against me and pointing at Gideon, who isn't moving, just standing still.

'Lincoln, look at me. Lincoln, just stop it.'

I stumble back with each push of his weight as he reaches for Gideon over my shoulders. *'I'm going to fucking kill you,'* he screams and I don't know what to do. My heart is racing and I can't think and I'm breathing fast and so I do the only thing I know to do when it comes to Lincoln.

I kiss him.

I kiss Lincoln hard on the mouth with both my hands still on his face and he's tense at first, he tries to pull back but I just push against him harder, my whole body pressed against his. Then I feel him move his body into mine. I can feel both his hands on my face and he kisses me back. Thrashy and hard and intense. And then I hear two things: my own sobbing and Gideon's footsteps as he runs away.

GIDEON

I don't know how long I'm outside before Ava appears. I'm crouched on the footpath outside the hotel trying to catch my breath. I'm sobbing. Trying to work out what the fuck just happened and what I just did. How could I have been so stupid? But seeing them dancing like that—it just turned my insides to lava and I felt completely out of control.

Ava touches my shoulder. I look up at her and she's panting. She's been running and her mascara is all over her cheeks. I stand up and grab her tightly. Holding on to her like everything depends on it. It feels like it does.

I don't know what's wrong with me, it was just when her name came out of his mouth, something snapped inside me and every ounce of my anxiety morphed into anger. Every bit of disappointment, confusion and embarrassment turned into white-hot rage. I can't say anything. I can't. I'm being fuelled by some other part of me. I'm shaking. I can't believe I hit someone. On purpose. I wanted to hit him. I wanted to hurt him.

'What just…I'm so sorry,' Ava moans.

'It's okay. It's okay. It's okay,' I say quickly, squeezing her, and she pulls away. Looks at me.

'Gideon, no. You should be angry.'

I nod, putting my hands on her face to convince her. 'I am angry.'

Ava looks confused and she speaks slowly. 'I kissed him.'

Those words sting every inch of skin. 'Yeah…but you didn't want to—'

'I—'

'Did you want to?'

'I don't know. No. But…' She pauses. 'I did. And you can't just pretend that didn't happen.'

'But I can't lose you, Ava.' I try to kiss her but she pulls away.

'Why aren't you angry?' Ava pushes me. 'You should be furious.'

'I'm just—'

'Gideon?'

'Because it's my fault. It's all my fault. I'm sorry. I'm sorry.'

'Why are you apologising?'

I need to tell her, convince her. 'Because I hit him. I shouldn't have hit him. If I didn't hit him then none of this…It's my fault. I don't know what happened, I saw you dancing and I got jealous and I'm sorry.

Let's just pretend it didn't happen.'

She closes her eyes and a weird sound, a kind of moan, slips from her mouth. She says, 'I can't…'

'What?'

'I can't do this anymore.'

'What?' *No, no. Not this. Fix it. I need to fix it.* 'I just…Please, Ava, don't break up with me,' I sob, screaming inside.

'I can't…'

She stops and this awful look of clarity pierces her eyes.

'We can't be together anymore.'

AVA

'We can't be together anymore.' The words come out of my mouth before I've even actually heard them.

Gideon freezes. His brown eyes widen and his lips part as though he wants to speak, but he doesn't.

I pace. I let the words fly out. 'I shouldn't have done that, kissed him, and I don't know why I did. I've been so happy; *you've* made me happy. Maybe I don't know how to be happy anymore. I think I am just—I'm scared of it because I feel guilty. I feel guilty because she is dead and she's not coming back and she wasn't happy and I didn't help her and how is it fair if I get to be happy without her?'

'You deserve to be happy, Ava.'

'Yeah. So do you. I mean—' I stop, trying to speak. 'I just...Gideon, you mean so much to me.'

'No.' He shakes his head, crying.

'I'm sorry. I don't know what I'm saying. I don't want to make you sad. And I have, and it's almost like that's inevitable right now and I just think—'

'Ava—' He stops me. We breathe heavy as we stand opposite each other. We're both crying.

I wait for him to say something, anything, but he doesn't. He looks so helpless and I start rambling again.

'Please, Gideon, tell me that you don't hate me. I couldn't cope with that. Tell me we can still be friends. Gideon? Please?'

GIDEON

Please? It hangs there in the space between us like honey dripping down the side of a jar, all thick and slow and heavy.

I don't want to break up. I don't want to reach the end of this conversation. I don't want her to leave and not call herself my girlfriend anymore. I feel like we've both just landed in this brilliant spot where everything is right and then *boom*. Wrong.

Ava doesn't want me. I think my body is in shock.

'Gideon?'

'Thing is'—I say the first thing that comes to mind—'that I love you.' I feel the poem sitting in the pocket of my jacket directly over my heart, mocking me. 'And I don't know if can...' I hear my voice rise, get louder. 'I don't know if I'll be okay, Ava. Not if this is the choice you're actually making.' I see her expression change but

I don't stop, I rant on. 'And maybe it'll be your fault if…
if something bad happens to me.'

Ava's face turns the whitest of white.

She shakes her head at me in a perfectly distilled
combination of pity and anger.

'How dare you?' she heaves from her chest. 'I can't
believe you would say that.'

What have I done? I didn't mean that, not even a
little bit. I just wanted her to seem hurt, to feel something like I was feeling.

Ava is disgusted. 'I thought I knew you.'

'Ava! I didn't—' I try taking two large steps to get to
her before the inevitable happens: she turns around and
bolts. She's around the corner and probably halfway
home before I can even open my mouth.

I look after her, gaping.

'Ava.' Talking to the empty air.

I spin around on my heel and punch the concrete
with all my strength.

•

I storm inside the house with my parents on my tail.
We've just spent seven hours in accident and emer-
gency to learn that I've broken a bone in my hand. I'm
now sporting a cast, and have an appointment with a
surgeon on Monday.

To their credit they tiptoed delicately around me at
the hospital, trying to get the details of what happened.
And they waited until we were close to home before
they let loose with their questions and concern, but I

can't deal with it. Not today. I just want to go to bed and not wake up till it's all over.

'You need to back off,' I yell, starting the march up the stairs.

'Mate, we're just worried,' Susan yells after me, and Mum stands behind her, looking like the physical manifestation of worry.

'You don't need to be so *worried*,' I yell, sitting hard on the stairs. 'Fuck! I'm not broken.' I wish they would say what they were really thinking. I wish they would tell me I've let them down or they're angry or whatever, but they don't, they just skate around the surface, too scared to rock the boat. Except I'm the boat and the waters are already pretty rocky, so they may as well go for gold.

'I just have a broken heart,' I say.

'And hand,' Mum says, her eyes welling with tears.

'And hand,' I say. I look at the cast. 'But I'm not fragile. I'm just sad.'

'Yeah, but—' Susan stops herself. Then she says, 'The last time you were sad…' And she leaves it there. Climbs the stairs and sits beside me.

And I realise what a giant idiot I'm being. They're scared of losing me. I know what that feels like now.

When I finally do get to my room to be quiet, I feel so completely out of it. Confused and sad and angry at myself. My hand hurts.

I look at my cast. I feel like shit for fucking it up with Ava, for saying what I did, for not listening to her.

Mostly, I feel like shit for being a bad friend. All I ever wanted was to be her friend.

I bite my lip and think about her, and my heart starts to race and my stomach hurts, because I realise there's nothing I can do. She can't get what she needs from me.

AVA

Everything is shit, but weirdly I feel okay. I feel sad about Lincoln. I feel bad about Gideon. I feel awful for ruining his formal.

It was like my brain just got sick of me not listening, that it was just like, 'ENOUGH,' and it went off, flipping metaphorical tables and showing me how we actually felt.

And then Gideon did some table-flipping of his own. Said some awful things and kind of…put the last piece in the breakup jigsaw.

Now all I want to do is talk to him, to debrief about everything that happened. I want to know what he thinks and if he's okay and I want him to make it better, to make me laugh. But he's the one person I can't talk to, because he's the one who made me feel like shit. And I'm the one who's made him feel like shit.

I don't know what I'm meant to do. I miss my friends. I feel completely alone.

But maybe that's the point: I don't know how to be alone. And I feel like I should know how to do that.

GIDEON

We talk about it in the end, me and Mum and Susan, after I've spent a couple of days in my room, marinating in my idiocy.

'I need you to stop freaking out and walking on eggshells around me,' I say. 'Tell me I messed up. Tell me I'm an idiot or something. Stop pretending you're not pissed off. You should be pissed off.'

'I am pissed off.' Susan nods.

'I'm not pissed off. I'm just worried,' Mum says calmly. 'Because we've been to the edge, Gids, I know what it looks like to not have you, and that thought is just fucking unbearable. So, you know. I do mother you and I do worry and I hear what you're saying but you also need to hear what we're saying. We love you and we're always going to worry about you and you need to just suck it up.' She pauses. 'You also need to not hit people like a stupid bonehead jock.'

'Shit, Gids,' said Susan. 'You made her say fuck. It's serious.' And that smashes the intensity in the air and we laugh about it, and eventually we get constructive.

We talk about what we can do better. We talk about my triggers and how this will affect my depression. We talk about me letting them in and not blocking them out all the time. About calling Robbie to get his advice, and also about finding a new therapist in town just so I can stay on top of everything.

We talk about changing my medication. They tell me they need me to be honest with them. I tell them I need them to listen to me, believe me and trust me when I tell them *I'm fine*. I tell them that I can't keep feeling like they're going to crack every time I do something that isn't sit in my room and be quiet. And I remind them that I'm not the same kid I was when I was fourteen. I've changed. I've grown.

I think about that later, on my own. Everything that's happened this week. Even apart from splitting up with my girlfriend and having my heart broken and acting like a massive douchebag, what I really can't believe is: I punched Lincoln.

Suddenly a smile cracks across my face. I HIT SOMEONE. I didn't back down. I reacted. I made a choice and I backed myself, even if it was a disaster and senselessly violent dickhead behaviour but whatever, I still did it. I did something, for once.

A weird wash of pride fills my chest and I laugh a

little. I didn't run away. I was *actually* brave.

Right now, even though I'm feeling a million things at once, I realise I'm okay. I'm gonna be okay. I've been braver then I ever thought possible this year and it's paid off.

This is how I think I want to be from now on. Brave. Doing more, being more. I'm so *sick* of being passive.

And I've got to keep sorting my shit out, because life is messy.

But fuck, it can be beautiful.

AVA

There's a knock on the door. My stomach flips, praying it isn't Gideon but hoping desperately at the same time that it is. I open the door and see the back of Lincoln walking down the front porch stairs, and there's a single gerbera in a bit of brown paper on the welcome mat.

He quickly spins. 'Hey,' he smiles.

'What are you doing?'

'Just wanted to leave you that.'

'Why?'

'No, no; no need to thank me.'

I look at the bright yellow flower and for a second I wish that this flower was from Gideon, not Lincoln. Go figure.

I want to be mad at Lincoln. I want to tell him to leave. I want to jam the flower into his chest and turn quickly on my heel and slam the door. But looking at him with his hands in his pockets and sunnies on, biting his bottom lip all shy, I can't do any of it. It's like my body is in direct conflict with my brain. My brain is all like tell him to piss off, but my body feels all the ties of the history between us, all these little cords connecting us together. They're impossible to break. He is a link to my past, to all of these feelings. He is central to most of my childhood memories and he is my link to Kelly.

'You've never bought anyone flowers,' I say.

'You don't know that.'

'Who, then?'

'Samia Jackson in Year 10. For Valentine's Day. I even bought her a teddy bear.' He smiles.

There's a pause. A pause long enough for some of those ties I thought I had cut the night of the formal to quickly reconnect, like some kind of wild vine that grows no matter how often you kill it.

'Why are you here, Lincoln?'

'Just cause, Aves.' He stops. 'Cause of this year, cause of it...all, yeah?'

I nod because I know exactly what he means. I think it too. I'm sorry we did what we did, that we hooked up when we didn't really want to, that we yelled at each other and said that awful shit. I'm sorry that I didn't tell him how I really felt about Kelly dying, that I didn't let him in. I'm sorry for what happened at the formal and for thinking that I could ever cut him out of my life. Most of all I'm sorry we let Kelly down.

I sit down on the step and Lincoln edges towards

me and perches tentatively next to me. We sit in silence for ages.

I notice the bruise that pokes out from beneath his sunglasses and I gasp, pointing at it. He takes them off and looks at me; the skin around his eye is all different shades of purple.

'We broke up.'

'I'm sorry.'

'No you're not.'

Lincoln scoffs and smiles. 'Boy can punch, though.'

We both laugh. Eventually it subsides and we're silent for a moment.

'Will we ever be friends again?'

'Were we ever friends?' He smiles.

He's right. We were never friends. He was always just Kel's brother and then we got complicated, but we were never friends.

'Can we be?' I ask and I mean it, and without even hesitating he looks me in the eye and he says, 'One day.' And I know he means it too.

'At a time?' I smile.

'Yeah, Aves, let's take it one day at a time.' He pauses. 'Everything got really fucking messy, yeah? I don't know much about anything right now. I'm angry *all* the time, at Mum and Dad, at you, even Gideon, but mostly it's cause I'm angry with her. *So mad.* I keep taking it out on everyone else, and it's shit. All of it.'

My eyes sting as I bite my lip and he takes a deep breath, holding it together.

'I'm just sorry.' He looks at the ground. I touch his shoulder and breathe hard.

'Yeah. Me too,' I say, and then we don't talk for a while.

'You gonna come to graduation?' he asks.

'How are you even graduating?' I smile.

'Pure fluke,' he shrugs. It's not a fluke, it's cause he's smart.

'Come?' he asks.

I shake my head.

'Why not?'

'Because I might tell everyone to get fucked.' I stretch out my legs and listen to Lincoln laugh.

'Come'—he looks at me—'as friends.' I smile and hold our eye contact for a moment and what passes between us is some kind of acknowledgment that things are going to be different.

I look away, nodding. 'What about your parents?'

'They want to see you.' He stands up, quickly squeezes my shoulder and starts to walk towards his car. Lincoln seems different, like something big has changed. I want to know why.

'Oi!' I yell and he turns his head. 'Why now?'

He smiles quick. 'Cause I watched *Lilo and Stitch*.'

'What?' I crack up laughing.

'*Ohana*, Aves.' And he nods, gets in his car and beeps the horn twice as he pulls away.

It's classic Lincoln to create meaning from something so random. He hasn't taken on any of the advice he's been given or shit that people have done to try and help him and in the end the thing that cuts through it all is a freaking Disney movie. *'Ohana' means family, and family means no one gets left behind*. I smile and feel pulses of happiness and relief as the knot that has been wound in my stomach because of me and Lincoln finally relaxes.

•

I'm sitting behind two girls who were in my year; one of them is crying and the other is trying to comfort her. She's crying about Year 11 being over and how she's 'so gonna miss the Year 12s cause they're so amazing'. It's taking all of my possible restraint to not tap her on the shoulder and tell her that none of them care about her and to stop being so fucking dramatic.

I sit next to Greg and Tina, who saw me waiting on my own in the carpark. My plan was to just sneak in at the last second and stand at the back of the auditorium and then sneak out again, but Tina saw me and walked over. I thought for sure she was going to yell at me, but she didn't say anything; just hugged me tight and kissed my forehead.

I looked at Greg. 'We've missed you, Aves,' he said.

I looked to the sky and willed myself to not cry, partly because I'm sick of crying and partly because I spent just that little bit of extra time doing my make-up today just in case I saw Gideon. I smiled and nodded and Tina held my hand as we walked into the auditorium and sat down.

One by one the Year 12s shake hands with Mrs

Bryan and get their certificate, and all pile onto these stands. I think about how they must be feeling right now. That's it. No more school.

I wish I was a year older. I wish I was standing up there with them. Mostly I wish I was standing next to Gideon and that everything was okay.

I keep my eyes locked on him from the second he walks onto the stage. I just stare, hoping and praying that he'll look at me. But he doesn't. Not once. Just stares at the back of the auditorium, looking like he always does. Curls hanging over his eyes, a dark shield against the world; a slight smirk that looks like maybe he's about to smile or vomit, it could go either way. He also has a bright blue cast on his arm. I wonder how he did it, how he hurt himself, and pray wildly that he didn't do it on purpose. A wash of guilt fills my chest. If he did do it on purpose then it'd be all my fault. Just like he said.

The Year 12s all march off the stage and take their seats in the first few rows as Marnie Albringer and some other music kids play guitar and sing some old song about friendship. The girl in front of me starts crying again because of some reason that I can't even be bothered listening to. I stare at the back of her head and my eyebrows do the talking, telling her in no uncertain terms that she's a dickhead. A couple of the boys hold up lighters and sway them in the air, but Mrs Bryan shuts that shit down pretty quickly, not before the entire auditorium has cracked up though, and Marnie looks like she's actually going to murder them. I laugh a little despite myself, mainly because Mrs Bryan's mouth looks like a dead-set cat's bum when she's pissed off.

When the song is over the stage-management kids run around setting up another microphone and Mr Neville says some cheesy thing about lighters and songs and everyone cracks up again. I look at all the award boards on the side of the hall, reading names of the kids who won in the past, half-heartedly listening to Mr Neville's next sentence.

'I'm not sure if many of you will know this, but one of our seniors, Gideon Franks-Myer, has had a bit of success in the slam poetry world this year.'

I feel my stomach lurch. Gideon will hate this, the attention. Will hate that they're talking about him and that they're going to make him get up and probably receive some stupid school certificate. I look to the front of the auditorium, scanning all the seniors for him, but I can't find him.

'Gideon has asked to perform an untitled piece today, so give him a round of applause.' Over a thousand pairs of hands collide together clapping as I watch him stride across the stage. I can't help it, my face cracks with a smile just at the sight of him. Then it fades. *What is he doing?*

Gideon stands at the microphone with his eyes shut. I don't think I'm even sitting anymore, more like squatting, hovering over the front of my chair staring at him. I feel nervous. I feel sick. A couple of kids a few seats up from me snigger and I stare at them. I want to get up and stand next to him and at the same time I want to run very fast out of the auditorium. He starts and it's like someone has punched me in the guts; all the air leaves my body as I thud down heavy in my chair. This isn't his poem. This is *my* poem. The one I sent him months ago. The one I wrote and gave to him and told him to read if he was confused. He's memorised it. He's performing it.

> she has a smile / she had a smile / everything changes between the 's' and the 'd' / she has / she had / she had so many feelings / but they took them away / couldn't feel anything / she'd say / what's the point in being young if you don't feel it? / like a million little fireworks exploding / she'd see the colours, but couldn't marvel at the lights / see them take over the sky / but could only focus on the dark.

> her chemicals and their chemicals tried to find a balance / she wouldn't stick to it / made her feel like she was flatlining / a life that was dull / no one can tell me that she didn't fight / like a ninja she'd stick to the shadows / a black-plaited princess fighting demons in the dark / she'd shift shapes before your very eyes / appearing and disappearing / tricking and flicking switches to a life only one-eighth lived.

> she's taken my secrets to her grave / taken my past with her / wrapped up in a carnation-covered cocoon / don't tell me / everything happens for a reason / she's in a better place / she was broken / such a waste / it's because we talk about her like it's a waste that we let her waste away / I'll never let her waste away.

> she lost / now we lose.

> she didn't want to end her life / she loved life

> she wanted to end her pain.

I can't move. Everything feels weird and it's not being helped by the fact that everyone in the auditorium is silent. Like dead quiet.

I inhale loudly, catching my breath, and it's only when I do that I realise that the whole time he was up there I was holding my breath. I glance at the people in the other rows and they're all just kind of stunned. Gideon nods and then walks to the side of the stage and applause erupts, like really truly erupts, and Mr Neville walks him back onto the stage and makes him bow and he smiles and bends his lanky body quickly and then a few people cheer and I don't wipe the tears away that I know are running down my cheeks because I'm stunned too.

Not because he did it, or because he was amazing, but because Gideon looks different. It's not confident; he still looks awkward and nervous, like he always did. It's something else. I turn my head to the side and look at Lincoln and Kelly's parents and they hold each other's hands tightly, they're both crying.

'Who is that boy?' Tina asks me.

'His name is Gideon.'

'Was he friends with Kelly?'

I nod and stutter out the word: 'Yeah.'

Mr Neville whispers something in Gideon's ear and he laughs, like really actually laughs with his whole body and I think I know what it is that's different about him. He looks like maybe, maybe he's not scared anymore.

•

I find him with his parents standing outside talking to Mrs Bryan. Susan smiles at me over his shoulder and taps his arm. He turns his head and sees me. I watch him swallow hard, turn back and whisper something to his mum and then stuff his hands hard in his pockets as he walks over towards me, looking at the ground. He doesn't seem nervous though, not like normal—just thoughtful, like he's thinking, a lot. Which really is normal.

'You were amazing,' some girl who is probably in Year 9 yells at him from a massive gaggle of girls as they walk past. I smile at him and he smirks, his eyes quickly darting over my shoulder to another group of kids talking and pointing at him. They wave, Gideon waves back, then he looks at me with his eyebrows raised. His expression tells me just how freaked out and weird he thinks all of this is.

I open my mouth to say something but before I do Gideon takes my hand and walks back towards the auditorium. He doesn't say anything, so I just follow. So happy that he's with me, that he's touching me, that he's going to talk to me. I think.

We walk in silence to the hallway at the back of the auditorium where there's no one around; he drops my hand and starts to pace.

'I had this whole thing rehearsed,' he says, 'this whole thing that I wanted to say. But'—he stops talking and pacing and looks at me—'it doesn't matter.'

'Me too.' I pause. 'I've tried to talk to you.' And I did, after Lincoln came over and we sort of worked things out, I wanted to do the same with me and Gideon. But when I went to his house Susan answered the door and told me he didn't want to see me. And with his stupid no-phone and no-internet policy there was no way to get in contact with him. I've started a million letters but none of them were right. I didn't finish any of them.

'I know.' He nods. 'I just couldn't.'

'I wanted—' I stop. 'I want to say I'm sorry. Again. I miss you.'

'I know.'

Neither of us says anything. All the times I've practised this conversation in my head and I can't remember any of it now.

'Your poem—' I say, but he cuts me off.

'*Your* poem.' He looks me in the eye, scanning my face for some response and I want to tell him that I feel angry at him for reading it in front of everyone and sad about what happened and happy that he kept it and proud of him for reading it out loud and that I still think he's amazing. But I don't. The only thing that comes out of my mouth is 'Why?'

'Why your poem?' he asks. I nod and he shrugs.

I know he knows why, and I want him to tell me but I'm just so glad that he's finally talking to me that I don't want to push it. So we stand there silent, with him kind of pacing on the spot and me with my eyes locked on his laces as his feet fidget awkwardly.

'Ava?'

'Yeah.'

'This is shit, isn't it?'

'Yeah.' My heart is pounding. It feels so violent that I'm positive if I looked down I'd actually be able to see my chest move.

'You told me to read your poem when I was confused, and I was. I guess I realised how confused you were, too. I mean, I did your poem for Kelly, sure. People here need to think about it, about her and what happened. But mainly I did your poem because I love it; there's parts that I think just summarise how I feel. About me and you.'

He breathes loudly again, and I can see in his face how hard that was for him to say.

Why is everything always so hard to say? I want to ask him which parts, and what he means exactly, and how does he feel about us, and if we can be friends. I want to ask him if the poem is the only thing he loves.

I want to ask Gideon if he still loves me. But I won't. Because the idea of him saying no is too freaking enormously painful and so I'd rather not know either way.

'Are you mad?' he asks.

'That you did the poem?'

He nods.

'No.'

More silence. He smiles and takes a few steps towards the door. I don't want him to go.

'I wish. I wish—' I pause. I breathe in deep, willing the words to come. 'I wish lots of things' is all I can muster, and Gideon smiles.

'I can't be friends with you for a while, Ava.' He mutters this and I'm positive my heart actually clenches.

'I respect you and your decision, and I get why you did it, but I need you to respect this decision too. I can't be around you or talk to you. Not yet.'

I bite my lip hard and will myself not to cry. I nod so that he knows I understand.

Gideon takes a deep breath. 'But I'll never let her waste away,' he says, looking me right in the eye. He nods his head, takes a big deep breath in and I think he's going to say something else but he doesn't.

What does that even mean? There's this feeling in the pit of my stomach that works it out before my brain does and I feel the size of that disappointment niggle at my insides but I don't let it in, not right now.

'Bye Ava,' he says as he pivots on his toe, turns his back to me and walks away. And I don't say anything.

AVA

It's a cloudy May day, it's been raining all afternoon, but it's clear now. There's even a little bit of sun. The clouds are so thick they take up the whole sky and everything looks a little yellow, like someone's picked the wrong filter and everything has a weird tinted tone to it. I've done four whole months straight of Year 12 at a brand new school and I haven't wagged once, or yelled at anyone, or told anyone to get fucked or had to see the principal or guidance counsellor. I'm amazed by my resolve, and the fact that I'm genuinely impressed with this effort makes me giggle to myself.

I take the long way home, stepping over puddles, kicking at crumbly gravel and flicking leaves on low-hung branches so the leftover raindrops leap off in excited bursts. I like walking the long way because I have to go past the park, right past the spot where

Kelly's family and I stood under the rotunda a few months ago, a year after Kelly died, and told stories about her. Laughing about the crazy shit she'd do and crying happy tears. We celebrated her life.

When Dad and I walked down towards the family that day Lincoln came up to us and hugged me so tight he lifted my feet off the ground. It felt awkward and normal and different all at once. We haven't talked much these last few months, but every now and again he'll text me some stupid joke and I'll reply. I think Lincoln and I will always have this complex bond, this weird not-quite-friendship, not-quite-family thing. I don't regret what happened between us. I'm not proud of it either, but it's okay.

I breathe through my nose and I feel, I feel, I feel calm. All the crazy feelings are still there, I know they are: the sad, the hurt, the anger, the confusion, the grief and the love. They're all there. Maybe they're in the box or maybe they're just not bigger than the sum of my parts right now.

I still go to Nola for therapy every fortnight. She likes the analogy of the box and likes to remind me that there's no right or wrong way to feel any of these things. It's just the choices we make in the name of these feelings that can get us into trouble. Sleeping with Lincoln was not the best choice. Breaking up with Gideon? That was the right choice even though it hurt like hell. I haven't heard from him since his graduation. Despite what he said about not wanting to talk to me I sent him one final letter. I worked out what to say. I needed to thank him for...well, for everything.

I told him I missed him at work and that Ricky did too. I told him about the moment when Ricky said to me, 'I don't blame you for doing the kissy-kissy in the cold room with that boy. He was nice. Quiet, but nice. A real catch.' I told him I was sorry for hurting him and that I felt awful about contributing to any more pain in his life, because he's experienced enough of that. I wrote about how amazing I think he is and how grateful I am that I met him because he made me laugh, and feel beautiful. I told him how I felt like it was because of him that I was able to realise that not everything in my life was a complete waste and that it was because of him that I wanted to sort my shit out, to be better. I thanked him for the incredible poems and for helping me pick up the shards of my smashed heart so that I could start putting it back together myself.

He didn't reply. Which I can't really blame him for. But still, it hurt. I assume he's moved away, gone to uni, is living his life—like he planned.

I've decided to really make a go of it this year and just see what happens. I still don't really know what I want to do. I'm hoping it'll become clear, as more time passes. Dad has started a counselling course so he can work on helplines talking to kids who are struggling. It sounds pretty interesting. Maybe I'll do that. I like that idea, of helping in some way, and god knows I'd be able to empathise. But then again, maybe I'll just work at Magic Kebab. Or maybe I'll be a poet. Who knows?

*

Ever since Kelly died people would talk to me about moving on. 'Ava, one day you'll move on and you'll feel okay.' I didn't believe them then and I don't believe them now. Part of me thinks that my life will always be kind of frozen in the moment that she died. Life as I knew it stopped then. Completely. Dead still, literally. When people would tell me that I'd move on it used to make me so mad—showed me quite clearly they had no idea what she meant to me. That she wasn't just my best friend, she was my soul sister. And that kind of love doesn't end. You can't just move on from that.

But that doesn't mean I can't move at all. Kelly dying will always define me in some way or another, but I can move forward. I owe that to her. Like I said: Kelly didn't want to end her life, she wanted to end her pain. Which she did. That means I can't let my pain end my life, I've got to live for both of us. I think that's what she'd want.

No. I know that's what she'd want.

When I get home, I kick open the front gate, reach into the mailbox and head inside. There's a pale blue envelope in with the bills. Addressed to me. I thumb the stamps for a moment before ripping it open, and take out a small rectangular card. I smile and breathe out. My eyes begin to do their usual welling thing, but this time it's a new feeling. This time my eyes are welling for no other reason than happiness. Real happy tears.

GIDEON

Dear Ava,

Why don't you text me sometime—you know, like a normal person?

My number here is: +44 7974 812134.

London sends its love. So do I.

Always.

Gideon

HELP IS ALWAYS AVAILABLE

If you or someone you know needs help you can seek assistance from one of these resources. Many have immediate support options including telephone, online chat and email services.

It's okay to not be okay. It does get better. Talk. You matter.

Love

Claire

www.claireandpearl.com

AUSTRALIA

Lifeline: 13 11 14
www.lifeline.org.au

Suicide Call Back Service: 1300 659 467
www.suicidecallbackservice.org.au

Kids Helpline: 1800 55 1800
www.kidshelpline.com.au

Beyond Blue: 1300 22 4636
www.beyondblue.org.au

Headspace: 1800 650 890
www.headspace.org.au

ReachOut: www.reachout.com

ACKNOWLEDGMENTS

My biggest and grandest heartfelt thanks to:

Everyone at Text for being so gosh darn lovely; in particular, to my editor, Mandy Brett.

Candice and Jen at RGM. The #LoveOzYA community.

Maree Keating, Harry Wallace, Mark Mackenzie and Wren Condren—thank you for your help and for telling me to keep going with this idea.

To all of the young people I've had the privilege of working with—thank you. TRACTION—you make me want to be better. I believe in you. Always.

Jacq, Heidi, Sam—best bests ever. Carley, Ari and Emily—thank you. Poppy, Tilda, Sid and Baby Burton—you can do anything, my loves. Dave, I will be eternally grateful for your brain, your encouragement and all of the giggles.

Nan, Granddad, Uncle Steve, Aunty Theresa, Liam, Anne, Cathy, Chris and Carla—thank you for your unwavering belief in me. I love you. And to my baby niece/nephew—I can't wait to meet you. Dad, I love you moo. Mum, my shadow and my queen—I am who I am because of you. Thank you.

Steve and Midge—I love you, and most importantly, I like you. My heart, always.

Lastly, to the @claireandpearl community—for being the sparkliest of them all.